THE PURIFIER

Andrew Beach Young

The Purifier is dedicated to my auntie Cathy Thomas.
I will see you someday in the Forest of Beauty...

ACKNOWLEDGMENTS

I would like to thank my mother, Susan Young, and my father, Russell Young, for their inspiration and help in the production of *The Purifier*. I would also like to thank Elizabeth Roberts for being my mentor, through prison mail, in bringing this story to the public eye. And lastly, Thank you Jesse Woodend, for designing this beautiful book cover for The Purifier.

CONTENTS

PROLOGUE

Michael Joseph awoke from a deep sleep with a hot face in need of a shave. He still wore the same tight-fitting jeans he had put on the day before. He could feel the button at his waist, jabbing an indentation into his belly as he pulled his torso upright. His face was flushed from the hours his head had drooped upside down off the edge of his bed. The beating pain in his temples undoubtedly resulted from the combination of a bad hangover and the blood rushing to his head. He had no idea how long he had slept. He felt like a murder victim caught cheating by his wife and killed in his sleep.

None of his early-morning realizations were uncommon as he told himself most mornings that he needed to stop drinking so much, nor was he surprised at the bottle of narcos he had knocked over, pills spilling onto his bedside lamp table among the accumulation of empty beer bottles. More empties were scattered throughout the rest of his apartment like candles in some unspeakable witchcraft ritual.

Micah who made up his own nickname at the age of 3 when he couldn't yet pronounce the l at the end Michael, felt sick and disgusted with himself, and his dirty and neglected apartment seemed to feel the same way—as if they were bound together in one single, miserable existence. He sat on the edge of his bed staring at nothing, the beeping of his alarm clock and regular chirp of his answering machine creating possibly the worst musical melody ever known to man or to alien life-form.

He had not wanted to leave his dream…and his father.

MICHAEL JOSEPH

Michael Joseph was on the shore once more. He was not be-wildered about why or how he got there; his mind brought him back to this place every few months, as though it were a puzzle with a missing piece he could never find. He saw himself walk-ing around a small island that protruded from the surface of the ocean, far out from any other neighboring shore.

His island was no more than a large sandbar with tall, hard-ened stalagmites rising throughout the center from end to end. In the distance, on the horizon, lay a much larger island, green with ancient-looking underlying layers of rock. It was beautiful! Was it his destination? He couldn't possibly know for sure, nor did he seem to care much. The ethereal feeling of this place was always enough to make Micah want to forget that he was dreaming and just stay there, deep, deep in his blissful sleep.

This time was extra special, because his father was here. Whenever Micah saw his father in his dreams, the sadness and loss he always felt when he was awake disappeared. The sun was in the late-afternoon position over the island, leaving shadows beneath his feet and hanging from the sandy rock pillars. His father also had his own shadow because, in Micah's dreams, he was alive.

There may have been some dialogue between them, but that wasn't important. For now, Micah just basked in the warm, happy feeling that he and his father were alone together in this otherworldly place.

This time, this dream, they walked along the shore. Micah felt no sense of urgency, no desire to try swimming back to any existing shore. Perhaps they had lingered too long, and the tide had risen. Now the ocean engulfed the island completely, but Micah had no desire to leave. This was their place.

Micah stood, watching his father gazing out on the water at the edge of the sand. His father's arms rested at his sides; he smiled as if to say, "Boy, isn't this great?" Yes, it was. Micah knew that his dad was there and that his dad knew he was. Is there anything better than that? He didn't think so. Dreams are one of human life's wonders. Although scientists have their research and theories about them, their deep meaning is concealed within the sleeping mind, and their deep truths are as unknown as death and the afterlife.

Richard Joseph was a great father to Micah, and a closer friend to him than anyone else he had ever known. He passed away a year ago to the day, and Micah still felt that they had unfinished business. Well, he thought that anyone who lost someone so close and so unexpectedly would feel the same. He didn't give a fuck what his psychiatrists told him about how to deal with his feelings of regret and loss and missed adventures with his father. "Life goes on," they said, "this too shall pass." "Stay busy," they said. "You'll get better if you join a grief counseling group." He hadn't been ready, and he missed his dad so much.

Micah shifted his eyes to a beer bottle with its contents sitting at midlevel. What was that fucked-up phrase his ex-girlfriend Janine used to use? "Micah, do you see the glass as half empty, or half full?" The answer was supposed to determine whether he was a positive or a negative person.

Micah felt a sharp surge of anger, as if the bottle was conspiring with all the righteous beeping of the bedside electronics to annoy him.

"Who the fuck says that? It's half full, and I'm still a negative person, you fucking swamp donkey!"

He grabbed the half-empty bottle from the table and flung it at the wall, smashing it. The noise didn't make a difference to his neighbors; he lived in the southern Arizona desert's version of the 'hood. The apartment rents were cheap and that fact drew a lot of people who were down on their luck, or alcoholics, or druggies looking for their next fix. He could already hear the abusive couple next door—whom he had never met—gearing up for their first fight of the day. Their arguing was becoming louder and soon there would be the banging of doors, accompanied with angry screams, before it all stopped when a car screeched its tires and drove away.

MOVIE BUFF

Micah shook himself out of it, stopped the alarm, and picked up the phone. Sandy, who managed the video rental store he owned in the town two miles from home, would be wondering where he was. The store was called "Movie Buff," a name he had chosen because he was a bit of a movie buff himself, but in the four years since he bought the land and building he had begun to hate working there.

The place was once a small pet store, and even though Micah had the walls power-washed and new carpet put in every year, the place never lost its everlasting smell of fish food and hamster shit. He had a total of maybe fifty customers a day. The store wasn't a Blockbuster, though it did have hundreds of movies they didn't carry—underground classics such as *King Solomon's Mines* that could never be found anywhere else. Micah and Janine used to watch a lot of movies and cuddle. He thought the store would impress her. She left him shortly after he bought the place.

Although he owned Movie Buff, he tried to avoid working there. Sandy, who loved her job, expected him to open the store every morning, lock up again and then reopen after lunch, and return in the evening to check on things and close for the night.

He thought he might make her smile today by giving her a key of her own for mornings like this when he woke feeling lethargic. He didn't have to bother listening to his phone messages this morning; it was eleven thirty, and the place was supposed to open at ten o'clock. Sandy was probably already back home by now. Fuck!

Before his phone rang once, he heard, "Micah, where are you? Do you know what time it is? Are you OK?"

"Yes, I'm fine. I'm sorry, Sandy. Give me twenty."

"OK, because that shipment of horror classics you ordered last month finally arrived as well as the billboard set-up for the new Batman movie. The guys have been waiting here for an hour Micah!

"Shit! All right, just give me ten!"

Micah splashed water on his face, hurried to his car, and drove the two miles to Movie Buff. As he pulled into the driveway behind his store—an oversized, perfectly square box of a building—he glimpsed his gloomy, unshaven reflection in the rearview mirror. At thirty-six, Micah thought himself ugly, but women seemed to think he was handsome. Today, his body smelled like fermentation, and he realized he had to take a shit. He would have to stink up Movie Buff's only staff restroom—Sandy's, really, all done up with her clean-girl touch. Just great! He thought about taking a few pills and getting a little buzz. At this time in his life, that was really all he had.

Micah felt guilty for abandoning his movie shop and preventing sweet Sandy from doing the job that he had given her—a job she was so thankful to have. The place looked clean and orderly, as Sandy always took the initiative to keep it that way. This was the first time Micah had actually looked inside Movie Buff for a week. He desperately needed to clean up his act, not just today, but in general.

He needed to do some things, and as badly as he wanted to send Sandy home for the day, he couldn't work in her place. Sandy wouldn't have it anyway. She enjoyed working at Movie Buff because it was like her home away from home. Micah had an idea there were problems at her actual home, although he would never pry into her private life. Sandy was a very pretty girl with a whip of long auburn hair, speckled green eyes, fair skin, and lightly freckled cheeks. She was about nineteen or twenty, or at least he thought she was. He never scanned her résumé to see just how old she really was.

Micah supposed that he should probably hire an additional employee, preferably a male coworker, to give Sandy a touch of security and safety. Instead, he insisted that she take the next day off with pay while he worked the counter himself. Micah wanted to inquire whether she had a group of girlfriends or a boyfriend to spend the day with, but he restrained himself.

Sandy was obviously curious about the offer, but she accepted, commenting that she would take her grandmother to lunch.

MYSTIC TEMPLE

M icah took off, lost in his thoughts and driving without any particular destination, until he found himself pulling into possibly the only unfamiliar store in this small town—the Mystic Temple. It was one of those places he passed by every day and never seemed to notice. Its purple neon sign and the erotic stone objects on display in the window were recognizable only as another distance marker between home and his pathetic self.

A couple of gothic punks sat smoking and fidgeting with a lighter on the cement curb marking one of the store's four parking spaces. The inside of the store was quiet and dimly lit, not much bigger than Movie Buff. It sold headpieces, a small collection of hemp clothing, incense, tobacco, and what Micah was really interested in: instruction on and equipment for—supposedly—contacting the dead.

The clerk, an old woman, gave forth the vibe of a person who understood things that normal people could never possibly hope to comprehend. She was small and very wrinkled, with skin the color of dark caramel. She seemed to float from out of the beaded ropes hanging in the doorway leading to the employee section in the back of the store.

She smiled, showing decayed teeth. An animal of some sort, probably a vintage fur, looking like it belonged in a zoo, hung from her shoulder. A necklace of fingers—or dried chili peppers, Micah realized on closer inspection—dangled from her scrawny neck.

"I am Jenny. How may I help you, kind sir?" asked the old woman.

"Well..." Micah's thoughts came into a dull focus on what he was doing. He didn't really know what he wanted. "You know, I think maybe I should come back," he said with a forced smile. He shifted to duck the old woman's gaze and walk out.

"Ah, so you wish to contact your father who has passed from this world and on to the next," Jenny said.

Micah caught his breath and turned to stare at the woman. He felt an uneasy sense of déjà vu, followed by an uncontrollable surge of anger.

"How could you know that?" Micah demanded.

"You told me with your eyes, young man," she said.

"Young man?" Micah began. He supposed he wasn't exactly old, but he felt far from youthful these days.

"No bother with that. What matters is that you must know you have a great gift—a gift very few possess, and one as old as the mountains of creation. You will not need a Ouija board to contact spirits, Micah. They will contact you."

"How do you know my name?"

"You can learn much about a person by peering through the windows of his soul," Jenny replied.

Micah looked at her, stupefied.

"Your eyes," she clarified, somewhat impatiently.

Micah forced himself to look into her own windows. It was a bad idea. Yikes! Who was this woman? How could she know so much about him? This was feeling creepy!

"I can help you enter the realm of the spirit world with these," she said as she handed him a bundle of foul-smelling incense, "but they can make you very sleepy, so do not use them in your car."

"How much?"

"Fifty dollars, sir," said Jenny.

Jesus! What a fucking O-Key-Dokey this place is, thought Micah, though he must have been really interested, or Jenny was possibly the best saleswoman he had ever encountered. He found himself handing the old woman the money.

As he began to walk out, Jenny said, "Even a Purifier has to pay for his products in my store."

Michael Joseph needed a drink.

THE PURIFIER

The rain purifies the soil as it purifies the soul. Looking out at a street or garden through glass pelted by soft droplets fills the heart with an emotion that is difficult to fully describe. As you open your window or step outside, you can smell God. Possibly the best part of childhood is to run out under the weeping sky and play games in the rain, innocent and free of guilt. It is a wonderful feeling to be a conscious life in a world that cleanses its inhabitants as often as it can. People in the deep rainforests, who live out days of rain around the clock, may not wish for it the way some of us do, yet they must be thankful. A purifier can cleanse the soul as the rain cleanses the soil, so that life can grow—and life is heaven.

Micah never believed—or disbelieved, particularly—in spirits. He did not have many memories of his mother, who had passed when he was three years old, of cancer, and he was not sure if the memories he had of her were his own, or a combination of his memories and the stories his father told him about her. But his father was the one who raised him, and was always there for him, and now he was gone.

Soon after his father's passing, he was content to feel his Dad's presence in his dreams. But as time went on, he was becoming anxious to know if his father was really there or just a figment of his imagination.

He had to get to the bottom of it. He wasn't sure how, but he knew he would be searching alone. His ex-girlfriend Janine had recently become engaged and moved away—not that he really cared anymore, but she was no longer around for him to talk to, and he wasn't going to call her. Janine had always been his sounding board. She was a great listener, didn't put up with any of his bullshit, and was also a sympathetic ear. Micah didn't know if he was a "medium," but he was about to find out.

On the way home from his adventure at the Mystic Temple, Micah stopped to grab a bottle of tequila and a couple of counter limes. If he ever got started on the road to recovery, he knew he would have to move. Henry's Liquor was almost attached to Micah's apartment building, separated only by a narrow alley that gave shelter to a couple of low-lifes who never seemed to go anywhere. Micah parked his car around the corner of the liquor store so that he could see it from the small balcony of his apartment. He wondered if the homeless guys in the alley ever pondered breaking into his car, though he doubted it. There were times when slouching around in his own piss and filth, half-decayed from too much drink, didn't seem like the worst idea. He understood depression better now that he was so depressed himself.

Today, however, Micah felt more motivated than he had all week. He entered his apartment and decided to clean it up a bit. Jenny had lifted his spirits by telling him he was a Purifier—whatever that was—and his place did not look pure. He took out the trash, vacuumed, showered, shaved, and combed his hair. He figured that if he was going to try out the incense in the hope of communicating with his father's spirit, he should make himself presentable for the meeting.

He took his pills from the table and flushed them down the toilet. Micah knew that his father would not want him taking the pills, and he honestly didn't want to develop a dependency on them. Drinking, however, had become a steady habit, and he was not ready to give that up yet. Nor was he about to try his first séance without a swallow of something choice.

Micah closed his drapes and unplugged his hard line. He poured a glass of agave tequila and rimmed it with a slice of the fresh lime. He hadn't eaten anything today, but what the fuck. He pulled a dismal group of wilted roses—eons old—out of a small vase he had on the table in front of his couch and threw them in the trash. He emptied the stinky yellow water into the sink, dried the vase, and filled its bottom with powdered laundry detergent. He placed the incense in the soap, stick sides down, lit the upper tips, and then blew out their flames. The incense obeyed with a silent puff of smoke.

He sat on his couch, took two long swigs of his tequila, and stared at the incense. He actually didn't mind the scent now, it seemed to grow on him and it smelled of rosewood and lavender, which dispelled the foul, stagnant odor that seemed to writhe throughout his apartment. He thought about a high school girl-friend he spent a couple of summer months with. They would sit facing each other on her bed, staring at each other and giggling as they passed a joint back and forth, incense burning between them to mask the smell of the pot. He remembered how fun it was, listening to good music that seemed to speak your thoughts and beliefs for you. Hiding from the world together, they were satisfied with a mere daring kiss on the lips. The sudden awkwardness they shared for a few short seconds was followed by a warm feeling of trust when they realized they both had the same doubts. It was OK because no one was watching.

Micah took another drink. The incense did have a certain calming effect, though it was no sedative—as he had half hoped.

He wondered if anyone else in the world was spending the afternoon this way: in an apartment, solo and half drunk, with no music, no television, and no Ouija board, hoping to find answers to his or her life. He supposed not, but he couldn't be certain—this world was a strange one.

For some reason, today, he felt he was making progress. He might be alone, but he was taking steps. Cleaning his apartment, shaving, and throwing away his pills were first steps, and he wanted to do more. Before he realized it, he was crying. Micah's tears came down like rain, streaking his face in wet ropes, stinging his fresh-shaven pores, and slowly cleansing away his pain. He knew he had been masking his deep sadness with anger and negativity, and he had gotten to the point where his mind and body didn't want to be depressed any longer. He sobbed and sobbed, letting it all out, crying his sins and regrets to his father and mother. Micah held his head in his hands and just let the tears fall. There was hope inside, and it was this feeling amid all of the many hopeless days he had endured that made him cry. He wanted to be happy again and excited for a better future, as he was before his father passed.

He remembered a day of fishing with his dad. They spent an afternoon on the ocean in their little boat. It was a hot day, and the sunscreen they slathered on seemed to burn worse than the sun. He could still feel that experience—the water churning, and the whitecaps lightly splashing the sea spray up on his legs, from time to time.

His stomach was queasy though he would never have told his dad. Not because he wouldn't have understood and made suggestions, but because telling would probably have led to a shorter day on the water. There was no way in hell Micah would chance an hour less of fishing with his dad.

They dipped beers from their cooler, talked about women, movies, and fish. A common bass or trash fish would surface on their lines every now and then, though they could never bring themselves to keep any. That was not the type of fishing day it was.

They happily threw fish back where they belonged so that they could breathe again, and live in their rightful place.. As the sun beat down and the day grew tired, they headed back to the harbor. Micah felt sad that it was over, even though his old 'Pops' was smiling and satisfied. That day turned out to be the last time he and his dad fished together.

Micah could hear the knocking on his door. It sounded as if it were coming from miles away. He lifted his head and wiped his face with his shirt. When he looked around the room, nothing had changed. No ghosts. The incense smoked quietly, as if to say, "God works in mysterious ways." He urged himself off the couch and to the door.

A petite woman in a pink sundress, no older than thirty, stood there.

"Hello?" Micah said.

"Sorry to bother you, but are you Michael Joseph?" she asked.

"Yeah, what's up?" he answered.

"I haven't got long, sir. Will you please tell Jim that it was true? He was right, and I'm sorry. I love him, and only him…forever."

"Who's Jim?" Micah asked, bewildered. "Miss, I think you have the wrong place."

"No, sir. Please. You are the only one," the woman said.

Maybe she had the wrong apartment. Maybe she was loaded. She kind of looked like it. He turned around to grab a piece of paper and a pen in case she wanted him to take a message. When he looked back, she was gone.

Shortly after, he got a call from Sandy at Movie Buff. She was crying hysterically. There had been a tragic car accident right in front of the store. She witnessed the whole thing and she was really shaken by it. A young woman had been thrown through the windshield into the road and killed. She was wearing a pink sundress.

JIM AND CHARLOTTE

Jim was a construction worker on a large building site just a couple of miles out of Tucson. He was the foreman of his crew, and was well-liked by his men because he always maintained a professional and respectful attitude toward everyone he worked with. Jim spent many hours working alongside the owner of the company, Steve—"Big Steve"—Marshall. Charlotte was Steve's daughter, and one day she dropped by his office with coffee and doughnuts for her dad and his office staff.

Charlotte was beautiful, in a homespun, wholesome way. She wore her golden hair long and tied in the back with a ribbon. It was love at first sight for Jim.

Charlotte's father liked Jim very much. He could see that Charlotte and Jim were made for each other. Two months after that coffee break, Jim and Charlotte were married in a simple ceremony at a small chapel near Charlotte's family home.

Those first few years were very happy. Jim couldn't wait to get home every night to be with his girl. Charlotte was kind, thoughtful, smart, and very loving. She made every day special with her adventurous spirit. She was always planning little surprises for Jim, like a candlelit picnic dinner set out on their back lawn, or theatre tickets to his favorite shows, or a baseball game and beers afterwards at their favorite bar. They liked the same kinds of things; rock music, scary movies, hiking, and sports, especially baseball. It seemed like they had an idyllic life. Even the hard work building their first little home together was fun.

But sometimes events can cause people to change in ways they could never have imagined. After Jim had worked for eight years at Steve's company, the housing market crashed, and Steve declared bankruptcy. Jim was out of a job—and due to the state of the economy, he had no new prospects. He stayed home while Charlotte waited tables at a restaurant downtown. Money was tight, and they argued nightly about their lack of income. Charlotte was forced to work six and sometimes seven days a week just to pay the minimum on their bills. She loved Jim more than anything, but she couldn't help feeling a little disgusted with him. She knew he was depressed, and although he had never been much of a drinker, she frequently returned home to find him drunk on the back porch. They hadn't made love in over six months. Jim didn't seem to notice much was wrong, but Charlotte started to become more involved in her life away from home.

That's when Charlotte made a mistake. One night, when she was waiting on her usual tables, she came across a classy-looking man eating dinner by himself. He was poised and polite to her when she took his order. His name was Elliot. He told Charlotte that he was in town on business. As the night grew late and the other customers left, Charlotte spent the last hour cleaning the bar. Elliot ordered a nightcap, and as she washed glasses and straightened the bar area, they talked. Since it was nearly time for her to be off, she decided to have one drink with Elliot. She couldn't fight her attraction to him.

The following night, Elliott came into the restaurant late when he knew Charlotte was about to get off work. He asked her up to his room for a drink. She didn't bother to tell Elliot that she was married, and he didn't bother to ask. She knew that she was making the wrong decision when she accepted his invitation, but she did it anyway. She called Jim and told him she was going to spend the night with her girlfriends from work. She woke in the morning with the worst heartache and guilt that she had ever known. She did not love this handsome man sleeping beside her. She gathered her things and put on her clothes piece by piece. Poor Jim. She knew he was alone at home, feeling guilty because she worked all the time. She had made a terrible mistake and would never tell him. She didn't wanted to lose Jim or hurt him.

For the next year, Charlotte and Jim tried to work on their relationship. Charlotte didn't see Elliot again. She had been infatuated with him and he used her for a convenient fly-in-on-business fuck.

Charlotte knew that Jim would have kicked Elliot's ass if he ever had the chance, but he didn't know about the affair. She thought he suspected *something*, but he never pushed very much about the night she hadn't come home. Charlotte could tell that Jim was trying to be extra kind to her. He jumped at every opportunity to please her, which made her sad. She told herself that she was a stupid slut, and that she should never have cheated on him when he loved her so much. Even if he didn't know about her affair with Elliot, Charlotte knew he was still hurting. His eyes held a sadness that she had never seen before in all the years she had known him.

Jim went back to work eventually, and Charlotte continued to work at the restaurant. She regretted what she had done with a passion. The secret she kept from Jim was beginning to destroy the deep connection between them, and she felt a distance growing. She wondered if things could ever be the same again.

One morning, Jim surprised Charlotte with a question. "Honey, I don't know what your answer will be, but I have a proposition for you."

Nervously, he said, "Charlotte, I want to leave this shitty little town and start over somewhere else. I have my bonus check in the bank, and we have a few thousand dollars saved up. Would you consider leaving everything here and coming away with me? We could drive until we find a new place—a new future—just the two of us. I've been thinking about this for quite a while. We'd be taking a chance, but things aren't so great here anymore. I love you, Charlotte. I want to try again."

Charlotte's eyes lit up like they used to when they were first dating. Without saying a word, she tackled Jim, kissing him with a passion that had been sealed in like champagne in a bottle. That night, her tears soaked his face as they lay naked and entwined. It had been so long, and it was now so good again. Jim's own eyes were wet with tears of joy. Charlotte loved him, and they would go away together.

They packed all they could into her old Thunderbird and started out the next day, happy and full of hope. Charlotte wanted to confess to Jim her secret, but she didn't think this would be the right time. Nothing would put a damper on this day. They would ride into the sunset together, and whatever lay ahead was OK for her as long as she was with Jim.

MICAH'S POWERS

Mind, body, soul, and spirit, these are the things that keep the human connected. The ocean, the hills, the trees, the animals, and even the moss-covered soil hold the essence of the truth that we seek. It is all part of one love and one passage, our place beyond existence and our place in the universe.

Micah could not bend reality with his mind, or set things on fire with a flick of the wrist or a turn of the hand. He could not bring the dead back to life or open doors without a key. He was a regular human—although not a normal one, because there is no such thing as a normal human. Nevertheless, Micah was powerful. He could see into the realm of the spirit world like an owl can see into the dark of night. He possessed an extraordinary ability to help the insect in the crevasse, the wounded in the wilderness, and the innocent prisoner in the dungeon. He had the ability to free ghosts from their purgatory. The gift he had was natural, and it was his alone. Micah was a medium—a medium and a Purifier.

After Sandy's call, Micah realized that he was still standing by his front door, the telephone loosely gripped in his hand. He thought that most people would be in shock, in denial, or simply chilled with fear when they understood that they had just experienced an apparition. Some might not even put it together. Micah knew what had happened, however, and he felt his soul begin to ignite with the knowledge of his purpose in this life. His apartment was not haunted—except perhaps by his own melancholy and acquiescence to its silence. The hall outside was not a portal for spirits. He knew that the girl, Charlotte, came to him for a favor.

He was most likely too buzzed to drive, but he splashed water on his face, grabbed the keys to his Volvo, and drove back to Movie Buff to check on Sandy.

When Micah approached the store, he drove very slowly. Only one police car had arrived, together with an ambulance. A fire truck sounded in the near distance. A wounded bicyclist sat dazed and bleeding on the curb, and in the street in front of Movie Buff he saw a red Thunderbird split up the front from hitting a nearby telephone pole. A man was slumped over in the driver's seat, and a woman in a pink sundress lay broken and motionless ten feet away. Her name was Charlotte, and she was dead now. Micah knew that much.

He parked his car and ran around the emergency techs surrounding the body. The policeman directed the fire truck company from behind the car, and Micah had a chance to slide in close to the window of the driver's side, where the man sat bleeding profusely from his head. Despite the miraculous energy of the emergency crew, Micah knew that the man in the car was not going to live much longer. He was close to death, but his soul was carrying a question of burden and yearning. Although Micah had already forgotten the name Charlotte's apparition communicated to him in his apartment, he sensed it now—not by the life that barely clung to him like a carelessly hung jacket slipping from its hanger, but from the stronger pull of his passing spirit. Micah knew what he had to do.

He spoke. "Jim? Hey, brother, can you hear me?"

Blood covered the man's forehead, and his eyebrows were unmoving. Yet he still managed to turn his eyes, thick with red and deep in shock, toward Micah.

"Jim, you are going to die soon."

The man grunted.

"Charlotte is going with you beyond this. You will not be able to speak to each other before you go, but together you will dream an endless loving dream. You will lie in each other's arms, and hear all of your favorite songs, and it will all be real. Charlotte has a last thing that she wants to tell you before you go with her."

Jim groaned.

"She wants to tell you that you that it was true, that you were right, and she is sorry, and that she loves you and only you.... forever."

Jim took a long, slow breath, and he was gone.

Micah rose from his crouch and glanced over at the mangled telephone pole. To its side, he saw Jim and Charlotte embracing each other with the most beautiful show of relief on their faces. As he considered the telephone pole that had taken two lives and the ghosts who seemed to twirl together now in a beautiful dance, he saw the simplicity of the world's biggest mystery.

The awkwardness of the situation actually made him chuckle. The couple glanced back at him. They didn't wink, wave, or smile their thanks, but they met his eyes for a long moment before they went back to their happy kissing. They smiled as they kissed, and in that moment a thousand words were spoken between the three of them. Micah could not have explained what he knew in a thousand words or a thousand years. He was a Purifier, and he had purified two souls this day.

SANDY

Love may come and go, just as leaves fall from their trees and float away on the blowing wind. A smile on a lover's face can be either a beautiful captured moment or a painful memory. The truth of our existence needs no words. It can be as simple as the look in a beloved dog's eyes as he tells you silently that love is all that matters.

Micah drifted away from the dead man in the smashed car to where Sandy stood on the curb in front of Movie Buff. She looked agitated, but basically OK. She stared at him with a strange look on her face. The policeman had not seen Micah talking with the man in the car. He noticed him now but didn't say anything to him. The fire captain dispatched his men to block off the scene with caution tape and cones. They would be here a long time, most likely the entire night, and this street was possibly the busiest in town. Micah imagined the police leaving flares all around the perimeter.

This had been a long day for him, and probably for Sandy as well. She burst into tears as Micah came closer to her. She had always been a little secretive about herself, not letting her emotions out into the open, but now she stretched her arms out to hug Micah. He knew for certain that the violent accident frightened her.

Without thinking it through, he said, "Sandy, you look like you need a friend, and I do too. Would you like to have dinner with me tonight?"

"Really, boss? Sure that would be so good!" said Sandy.

As she looked up at him, the tears near her eyes dried. She was so cool. He liked her, even though he had never really taken the time to get to know her—she was just his employee. He hired her six months earlier, on the very same day she came in to ask about his hiring sign. She was the first person—actually, the only person—who had ever come into the store to ask about the job. She was always on top of things, organized and on time.

She was also, Micah realized with sudden clarity, very pretty. When he looked at Sandy now—at her tear-streaked cheeks, peachy and freckled—he found himself fighting a feeling of attraction. He needn't fret, he assured himself: she couldn't know what he was thinking. Besides, other than his old buddies up in Phoenix— whom he had not seen in over a year—she was his only friend.

JEREMY

The orange glow of the Arizona sun sank to half a dome at
the edge of the world as the sky turned to violet and the temperature began to drop. At eighty-six years old, Jeremy was afraid
to die. He watched the beautiful sunset until the sun disappeared
over the horizon, wondering how many more of these he would be
blessed to see. His nearly century-long life seemed to have flown by
as fast as a single day's passage from dawn to dusk.

Jeremy seemed like such a young person's name. He remembered, as if from a lifetime ago, how his name sounded on a woman's tongue, pretty and delicate, and her pride in saying it. Now his
eyebrows were overgrown, white and bushy. His hair had turned
white around the baldness on top. The beard on his cheeks, now
rough whiskers, was not worth shaving. His body, once well- mus-
cled from football, was fragile as a porcelain doll.

All these things he accepted and understood. What he didn't
understand was why, if it all had to end, he or anybody was given
such a gift only to have it taken back. Why take away the joy and
the sadness, the good and the evil, the sweet and the sour, the

love and the laughter. Jeremy loved it all; he loved his life and his memories, though he wished he could remember more.

There was a time when he felt confident in his knowledge of things. As a young man, Jeremy exceeded his parents' expectations, graduating ahead of most of his companions in his college classes. He enjoyed a successful career in journalism, traveled the world and brilliantly documented his experiences. He was an author. He had a wife, a successful marriage, and he watched as his son came into the world.

He also knew a hundred others who had left it. He felt pain at the passing of those he loved, and he felt remorse at some of their funerals. All his buddies had dropped, one by one over the years, and he often joked about death with them to ease their fears. They knew there was nothing they could do to stop time from having its way with them in the end.

But Jeremy never truly comprehended death until his wife died. Jeremy and his wife, Margaret, were married fifty-two years. They loved every waking moment together. He didn't understand the finality of death until she was gone. There were no more home-made breakfasts with the sausage cooked the way he liked it. There was no longer that deep-red lipstick stain on any of the glasses. He missed hearing her cheerful laughter and her musical voice. He was so lonely. Although he never believed in ghosts, he now hoped that Margaret would haunt him and give him one more smile to let him know that all was well and that she was waiting for him. But she never did.

THE DEMON

The demon lay still, taking deep, slow breaths in the darkness underneath the Arizona desert and thinking of the Purifier who remembered nothing of him. The centuries had passed, crawling and sluggish as a snail in this ungodly place. The mere thought of surfacing gave him chills of pleasure up his spine—like the hiss of the snake. He would take the form of a human man this night, make himself as unseen as possible in order to study this Purifier's every move and savor his smell. He would walk lightly on his feet and not disturb the insects on the sidewalk. He would follow the Purifier and hope for a place under his bed, where he could hide like an insignificant spider. The time was near. The demon climbed up a sewer pipe, the pads of his hands and feet sticky like those of a poisonous frog. Above ground, his eyes scanned the wall, gleaming a reptilian jade in the darkening sky. He took his perch on top of the roof of a place called Henry's Liquor. His toes curled over the edge of the adobe plaster as he inhaled through the flared nostrils of his pointed snout, savoring the ruddy toxins in the air of this human town. The demon felt the wondrous heat of the sinking sun on his pale flesh once again and molded his face into a devious scowl as he patiently waited.

A Purifier was like the hand of God, with the natural power to free each spirit from its everlasting sadness. Purgatory was a place where the souls of the dead could linger for years and years, not knowing how to cleanse themselves and be lifted to the heavens. A Purifier was like a scout from God, just as a demon is a scout of Lucifer. He or she could enter the realm of the spirits and relieve them of their unfinished business. Some would say that a Purifier was a breaker of rules, but a Purifier wouldn't care; it would take any punishment it deserved. A Purifier was a soldier without an army. Its sole purpose, in its time left on earth, was to help those dismal beings trapped in Purgatory.

Micah was a rare source of greatness and good. But where there is good, there will always be evil. Evil is always watching. The demon would make Micah remember that.

GRANDMA AND ROBBY

Sandy lived about five miles from Micah. The small town they lived in was surrounded by desert and farmland. Night was setting in just as he arrived at Sandy's rustic little house. The one-story wood-frame home sat on the outskirts of the town, out by itself near a small gathering of trees. After their strange day, he hoped they could both take a short break from the real world and enjoy each other's company.

Dim light came from the front room windows. The dark engulfed the trees behind the house, and the tall grass around it looked like a swallowing shadow. Micah stepped up on the porch and knocked on the front door. Sandy answered, and he stared at her, taken aback by her loveliness and the soft scent of her floral perfume.

Her eyelids fluttering like butterflies, she said, "Hey, boss! Hold on two minutes, OK? I'm trying to get my little brother to go to sleep. Would you like to come in and sit on the couch?"

"Oh, sure, yeah. Take your time, Sandy. I'm not in a hurry."

"Cool," she replied and disappeared into the hallway.

Micah sat on a couch covered in a leaf and rose design. The carpet showed stains in several places. He looked around the room to the kitchen and dining table, where an older woman sat quietly sleeping, a brandy bottle and glass at hand. He started, thinking for a moment that she was dead. She appeared to be about seventy years old, and he wondered if a drink put this woman to sleep more often than not. The brandy looked really good, and for a moment he thought about stealing a swig.

Sandy's voice called to him. "Hey boss, could you do me a favor and fill that pot in the sink with water and bring it down to Rob's room. We're in the second room down the hall on the right."

He went to the kitchen, filled the large roaster pan with tap water, and carried it into the bedroom. The air was thick and smelled sour. A boy of about twelve sat on the bed, a thermometer in his mouth. Sandy crouched next to him setting up a humidifier. She glanced up at Micah, making an obvious attempt to hide her worry. She glanced back at her brother. His pale skin looked clammy.

"Robby, I want you to meet my boss, Micah."

"Hey, Micah! I'm Rob. Are you taking my sister out?" he asked, smiling.

"Well, that was the idea, but I'm not sure now, man. You don't look like you're feeling that great," Micah replied.

Sandy gave a muted sigh, not taking her eyes off her brother. "Are you going to be kosher, Robby, if I go out for a couple of hours? Your fever is up a bit, and Grandma's passed out again."

"Oh, come on, Sis. You never go out at night anymore. I'll be fine." Robby said.

Rob didn't look fine to Micah, and he knew it would only be right to change his plans with Sandy. He thought the kid might need a little fun food, and he came up with a suggestion before Sandy could call the whole night off.

"Say, I've got an idea. Would it be all right with you two if I order us some pizzas and kick it here for a while and eat with you guys?"

He didn't know them well, and now that it was out, his question seemed a little awkward. To his surprise, though, Sandy and Rob were delighted. Sandy's eyes met his with a secret *thanks*.

Rob yelled, "Hell, yeah!"

Micah knew he had scored points with the small family. Sandy told Robby to rest until the pizza arrived, though Robby was smart and old enough to have done that without being told. He probably felt that he had screwed up his older sister's date. Micah's suggestion was perfect.

As he turned to follow Sandy into the living room, he saw Rob give him a wink.

"Would you like a drink, boss?" Sandy asked as he plopped down on the couch.

He liked the languid way her body moved as she headed to the cabinet for glasses.

"Yeah, sure. Do you have any alcohol?"

"Well, duh. Did you think I meant a glass of milk?" she asked as she pulled out a bottle of cheap wine. Her smile was youthful and completely sincere, but somehow a little sad too.

After they poured their wine, Sandy phoned in an order for two pizzas with a side of hot wings, and soda for Rob.

Relaxing on the couch with his glass of sour wine, Micah realized how really beautiful Sandy was. They talked for a while and shared a cigarette on the porch. The grandmother slept the entire time.

Sandy told Micah that her mother died in a car accident. That was why she had become so hysterical earlier in the day—it brought back so many painful memories. She and Rob never knew their father, so her grandmother stepped in to take care of them the day after their mother's death.

Lately, however, most of Rob's care had fallen to Sandy. "Grandma is depressed a lot," she said matter-of-factly. "Once she starts drinking for the night, I pretty much take care of everything."

Micah felt bad for her. He wondered how she had managed to work so much.

"Rob got really sick with pneumonia a couple of months ago," she explained. "He seemed OK at the last doctor's visit, but he looks like he's getting worse again, so I've scheduled an appointment for tomorrow."

Outside, smoking another cigarette, she asked him, "Micah, what were you saying to that man in the car today?"

He hesitated for a moment before saying, "To tell you the truth, a strange thing happened to me today."

He told her about his longing to contact his deceased father and how he used the strange incense purchased from the Mystic Temple in a séance.

"I used the incense to help me meditate so I could talk to my father. Well, the part about contacting my father's spirit didn't work, but I *did* talk to a woman named Charlotte."

"Wow! You mean like clairvoyance? That's incredible!" an enthralled Sandy exclaimed.

"No, it was more than that. It was like I already knew, kind of like I'd been expecting it to happen for a while."

In the moonlight, Sandy's eyes sparkled like dark green jewels. The sky around them was now thick and black, and beyond the brush at the front porch steps, the air was completely dark.

"Expecting what to happen?" Sandy asked.

"You know, I'm not really sure. Something I've hoped. This might sound crazy to you, Sandy, but I think I can—connect with the dead, somehow. Maybe even more than that."

Sandy looked searchingly up at Micah. He felt like he was seeing her for the first time. She did not seem to be judging him for the strange truth he had told her.

"Wow, that's cool."

Now it was his turn to ask her a question of his own. "How old are you, Sandy?"

"Hey, I thought you were psychic," she replied.

Oh, touché, thought Micah. "Not psychic, clairvoyant. Remember?"

"I'm twenty-five," she said with a smile.

They had probably read each other's minds. He felt a sense of relief and of nervous challenge all at once. He was attracted to her, but he didn't want to make things weird with his only employee at Movie Buff. He was thirty-six, but perhaps the age difference wouldn't matter to Sandy...They sat in silence for a few minutes until their peacefulness was interrupted by headlights coming toward them.

"All right! The pizza's here! We never get pizza. I can't remember the last time we did," Sandy exclaimed.

He knew they had come close to kissing—out of sheer lust, the wine, the cigarette smoke, the darkness...She probably wanted to just as much as he did, or at least he hoped so.

For the next three hours, they gobbled down pizza, drank sodas and wine, and played a game of Monopoly with Rob who was winning and who looked happy. Micah had the idea that life hadn't been too kind to the boy lately. The thought that he was contributing to Rob having some fun warmed Micah's heart.

A little later, when Robby was focused on the game, Sandy placed her hand on Micah's arm and then moved to his hand. She seemed completely comfortable doing so and although Micah was surprised because he didn't want to seem too bold in front of Robby, he liked the warm feeling of her hand in his and gave her hand a soft squeeze back. When the game was over and the little party ended, Rob dismissed himself, and Micah made his way to his car. He supposed he could have given Sandy a good-bye kiss, but the night had already included everything he could have hoped for, and possibly more.

She embraced him with a warm hug and said, "Thanks, Boss. Next time, we're going out!" She paused and added, "I hope Robby gets better soon. He's been sick too long."

Micah smiled down at her and wished her luck with the doctor's visit the following morning. Little did he know that his night was just *beginning!*

THE FOREST OF BEAUTY

The Temple of Purgatory was hidden in the forest of the mind. Not a soul knew how long it had been there or how it had gotten there in the first place. It stood in a forest so dense with greenery that it was invisible from a distance. The land on which it stood was in a dream within a dream. It was mystical beyond comprehension.

The trees that soared up from the moss-padded ground around the temple engulfed the earth beneath them with magnificent roots, winding and brilliant red. Their branches stretched themselves out for miles, and their green leaves created a thick moisture in the air, so pungent that it seemed to combine the sweetness of all the pines and grasses and peppers found in nature.

Plants sprang up from the dirt without a care, sprouting flowers of every color imaginable and creating intricate designs with their foliage. Pools of all shades of turquoise and blue, magical emeralds glowing from their depths, were spaced sporadically throughout this Forest of Beauty.

Creatures were scarce in the forest, for life there was a creation of the mind. Deer passed silently through the trees, knowing that they were safe and free to feed from the earth, drink from the pools, and search for the love of others of their kind.

They did not have to fear the white wolves of the forest, because no killing occurred here. There was no need or want to harm another. The fluffy white wolves were beautiful, and they did not eat meat as the wolves on earth do. They were the loving spirits of the Forest of Beauty, and they lived there to lead the way if one needed them.

Huge butterflies flitted through the air, and flower petals floated along with them. The Forest of Beauty was a jubilee of fascination, a fantasy far from reality. The Forest of Beauty was real. Within its depths stood the dark Temple of Purgatory and all the souls it imprisoned, all of them waiting for the Purifier.

SAMUEL AND CHAD

Samuel Snyder was a devoted police officer. He became a policeman at the age of twenty-two and was now forty-five years old. He taught himself to work hard, and he thrived on helping his community. In his quest to help others, over the years, he witnessed many ugly things in his work. Once, he found a crying baby alone and scared, screaming and crawling around his mother's feet as she lay dead from a heroin overdose. He watched numerous bodies being scraped from the asphalt, the aftermath of deadly freeway collisions. Witnessing so many tragedies hardened him throughout the years, and though deep down he only wished to serve justice, the residents of the city were afraid of him because of his reputation for being tough and unyielding.

Eventually, the worst thing that could ever happen to a man happened to Sam—and he blamed himself for it.

Sam had one son, Chad, whom he loved more than life itself. He only wished the best for him. However, when Chad became a teenager, he began to have problems that Samuel couldn't understand. He would often answer Sam in a defiant tone. Sam's wife, Shawna, pleaded with him to ease off their son a bit; he was at the age where he would, out of sheer defiance, act out in ways that his parents would not be able to stop.

"You need to understand that he's growing into a man, Samuel. He'll have to live and learn things for himself—whether you want him to or not!"

"Yeah, yeah, yeah. You sound just like him, Shawna. Do you think I'm going to let my only boy turn into another fuckup like those cretins I deal with every day?"

The conversation did not end well. Just as Samuel's rage reached its highest point, his son walked through the sliding glass door of the family room and right into the argument.

Chad sported baggy clothes like those of a ruffian, and his blond hair lay matted into locks. His eyes were swollen and blood-shot from pot smoke. He tried to avoid his father by walking through the kitchen and up the stairs to his bedroom, but it was too late for that.

"Where the hell do you think you're going?" Samuel growled.

"Away from you, bro," he said without raising his head. Chad could hear his father's angry tone and knew from past experiences, that he should have answered differently, but it was too late now.

That was the wrong thing to say. Samuel staggered toward his son and whipped him around with incredible strength.

"I am not your fucking bro. I'm your father!" he yelled.

"Da-a-d, please, just leave me alone!" Chad cried, tears in his eyes.

"You smell like fucking dope again, you sonofabitch."

Then Sam made an unconscious decision. He swung at his son, first across the right ear and then the left. He hit him until his wife scratched and clawed at the back of his head and neck as furiously as a lioness protecting her cub. Samuel swung around and hit her, too. They screamed and cried as Sam completely lost control.

At some point during the argument, Chad escaped the violence and left the house. He would never return.

FATE

Four years passed. Samuel was promoted to the head of the narcotics squad. There was an increase in drug related crimes in a couple of parts of the city, and Samuel's highly armored unit was specially equipped to go into dangerous situations first, ahead of other emergency vehicles.

Since Chad's disappearance, Samuel had become a ruthless machine at work. He slowly gave up every sentimental thing that made his life worthwhile. Shortly after Chad left, his wife divorced him. She might have hoped for Sam to make an attempt at reconciliation, but he didn't try to keep her in his life. He let her go like a dandelion in the breeze—after pulling every one of the last love petals from its stem.

Samuel took all of his son's possessions and pieces of furniture out of his bedroom and left them at the curb with a free sign on them. He even took his dog to the pound—like the animal was a stranger in his life. After his boy left, Samuel picked up the shit the dog left in his backyard with a grimacing scowl, as though the dog had done it to displease his master. After giving the family's best friend to the pound, he sat down and cried.

Samuel hated every second of his life between work shifts, because he had to spend them in the lonely house. He no longer cooked: he survived off frozen dinners and fast food. The memories of his life before would make most people depressed. All they did for Samuel was make him hate. Being a cop gave him the power to vent his anger on the victims of society in his small city. He became a monster—a monster with the law on his side.

Samuel got a call one afternoon regarding gang activity and possible drug dealing on the southwest side of the city. He drove through that area about twice a week to ticket people for loitering around the apartment buildings—this particular area was notorious for drug dealing. The city wasn't known for any big-time gangs, but Sam knew that the ones behind the scenes, without a name known to the police, could be the most dangerous. He was aware that the detectives' unit had been investigating two unsolved murders not far from where the call had come in, so he and his well-armed companions showed up at the scene with extreme caution.

Samuel and four of his elite team quickly moved around a corner and onto a path which led between the two buildings that held all the residents at that street address. The place was fairly large, with at least twenty different apartments in each building. People stood outside. He heard three different babies crying.

A middle-aged Asian woman came running down the staircase toward Samuel with her hands up and a frightened look on her face.

"He shoot gun! He have gun!" yelled the woman.

"OK, show me where," Samuel said as his men drew their pistols.

"Numba twenty-eight. Up derr, up derr." She pointed to the top of the stairs.

Samuel guided his men as they ran up the staircase, taking a shortcut by jumping over newly planted stubs of palm trees.

When they reached number twenty-eight, Samuel ordered his men to hold back, one at the stairs, one on the wall, and one braced against the other side of the door's entrance. The screen door was cracked open about six inches, and Samuel could see that there were no lights on inside the apartment. He pushed the door open slowly with his booted foot, hand steady on his pistol. In the dim light, Samuel could see a man with dark hair down to his shoulders standing with his back to him. He could also see the body of another man sprawled on the floor in front of him. They both held guns, though the man on the ground was still. The scene was eerily quiet.

"Put down your weapon, sir," Samuel said, keeping a safe distance.

"Ha, look who it is. Just leave me alone, man," said the figure, his back still turned and his gun held loosely at his side.

"Yeah, it's the police, you fuck-head. Now put your gun down before I blow your fuckin' head off," yelled Samuel.

"Why do you always have to call me names?" the man asked, turning slowly to face Samuel. His hair hung over his thin face, and his eyes—glassy with drugs--were as swollen and shadowed as those of any junkie. His skin stretched tightly over his face.

"Chad…oh…oh…my God!" Samuel stuttered in disbelief.

Before Samuel could do anything to help his son, Chad lifted the barrel of his own handgun to his head. "You never loved me," he said, and pulled the trigger.

The left side of his head, hair, and face seemed to explode against the wall. Blood splattered in a mist as he fell onto the carpet.

Samuel watched as tremors ran through his son's legs from the trauma of the aftershock and then as his entire body shook with the certainty of death. Only then did he realize that his men were holding him up by his armpits. He pushed away from them as rage and a fierce sadness filled his heart.

"No. God, No! Not my son. My baby!"

He crawled over to the body of his boy, all his hate and anger replaced by the worst feeling a man can experience. He held Chad in his arms and all at once felt the deepest love, regret, and excruciating pain. It was, at the same time, a sick redemption and the utter loss of salvation. He raised his eyes to the ceiling, and as he began to count the cracks in the paint, he lost consciousness.

Later, Samuel learned that both Chad and the dead man, Marley, were heroin addicts who dabbled with dealing small amounts of the drug. The incident had most likely begun as an argument over money or dope. It was an unfortunate mistake, and a tragedy that left Samuel completely hollow.

THE DEMON APPEARS

As Micah returned to his Volvo for the drive home, he felt butterflies in his stomach. He realized that it was the first time in many years he had felt that way after spending time with a woman. He wasn't sure if Sandy felt the same way, but he thought it was possible. How could two people share such a lighthearted night and not notice the impact they had on each other?

He had wonderful memories of Janine, although thinking about her for too long was always painful. He remembered walking along the coast in San Diego together, and the way the ocean rushed around her ankles making her shriek in delight at the surprise of cold water on her skin.

What Micah cherished most about Janine was their closeness and ability to talk to each other so easily. Sometimes it felt as if they shared one soul. Nothing else seemed to matter when they were in each other's company. He didn't even have to think about the things he said to her. When they were happy, his words—and hers too—were only loving things. He could be himself without the worry of being judged.

Now he wondered if she had grown to feel as close to her new man as she had with him. He wondered if she was having better sex with him. *Probably*, he thought. Micah hated the fact that every time he pictured her having an orgasm with another man, his own penis began to swell with heartbreak.

"Bitch!" he muttered to himself.

He realized that he had not yet started his car. Even though he was parked behind a stand of tall grass, out of view from Sandy's front porch, he should get going.

He had the strangest sense that he was being watched—*by the eyes of the night*, he thought, whatever that meant. Anyway, it sounded right. He was probably just feeling tipsy after drinking too much cheap wine with Sandy. The ride home would be a little adventure: he would have to drive extra carefully.

He fired up the ignition and started out at a steady pace. He lit a cigarette and flipped through radio stations, coming to rest on "Self-Esteem," by the Offspring, a song about a guy who couldn't let a girlfriend go, no matter how many times she broke his heart. He smiled. It was one of his favorites.

Micah rolled down his window for air and looked at himself in the rearview mirror. Over the last few days, he had begun to feel strangely powerful, as if a new energy coursed through his veins, and his physical body seemed to have strengthened. He was buzzed, but he didn't think that accounted for the metallic glow his dark eyes had taken on. The powerful music, the extraordinary experiences of the last few days, the thought of Sandy's smile, the alcohol in his veins, and the loneliness of the road ahead all gave him a wonderful feeling of euphoria.

He drove along a stretch walled in by tumbleweeds and sagebrush on either side, the moonlight providing very little extra luminescence to the light from his headlamps. The road was quite dark, and he felt quite drunk.

Before he could really process it, a dark figure appeared ahead of him—a man standing directly in his lane, about twenty feet in front of him. Micah swerved to avoid him, and the old Volvo veered down the slope to the right of the road, coming to a bumpy halt with its driver's side pressed against a furrow of dry brush and tall weeds.

Micah slowly released his tense hands from the steering wheel and felt around his upper body under the seatbelt. He had hit his head on something, maybe his door, and he could feel a small trickle of blood running down his nose and cheekbone. He shivered, remembering the bloody scene and how Jim looked earlier that day.

The driver's door was jammed, and grass stuck through the open window. He thanked God that he had remembered to fasten his seatbelt, even though it now held him tightly in place. His airbag didn't deploy as it should have. A week old cup of McDonald's soda sat in the cup holder. He had only sipped enough of it to make room for the handful of soggy, ketchup-covered fries inside. The mess was spattered all over his neck and down his shirt.

The sleeping black night pressed in around him. He could not unlock the seatbelt. In between increasingly frantic efforts to extricate himself, he heard what sounded like the slither of a snake. Micah hated snakes, and as he listened, the slippery, unearthly sound grew louder as it approached the car. He shuddered, holding his breath.

He recalled the man he saw in the road, causing him to crash. Was there a crazy guy lurking in the brush, someone hoping for excitement or death, waiting in the dark for an oncoming vehicle? He shivered again, in bewilderment and fear.

He heard something crawl up the back of his Volvo, the vehicle moving under its weight. Black fingers curled over the edge of the open window.

He stuttered in horror, "Hel…Hello? I'm hurt."

The hand became a long, slinking arm as the creature pulled itself to the bottom of the window. Its voice sounded impossibly low, the tone hollow and horrible.

"The Purifier…at last. Won't you be so kind…as to come with me?"

The demon shimmied through the window, one terrible limb at a time, and placed his scalding hot hand on the top of Micah's head. Micah screamed in terror.

LORD RAPTOR AND
THE TEMPLE

Micah awoke, the left side of his face pressed flat against what felt like carpet. The material was very soft; whoever owned it must have had expensive taste. He opened his right eye and saw a large rug spread beneath his body, decorated with numerous different shapes. He felt immobilized. From his position on the floor, he peered around at his immediate surroundings and realized he had no idea where he was.

Suddenly he remembered leaving Sandy's house, the car accident shortly after, and then the horrible nightmarish creature crawling in through the car window and seizing him by the head. Micah recalled feeling absent from his body and falling into oblivion, controlled by an alien force.

He pushed up from the floor, finding himself in a very large room. The ceiling must have extended twenty feet above him to a roof of beautiful stained glass. Looking more closely, he was able make out the devil, a group of battling angels, and a human soul between them. Light streamed through its colorful panes, coming down in bright rays.

He looked around the room and noticed a wall of polished cedar cabinets. The rug where he had awakened lay on the floor next to a large, soft bed, its headboard carved with images of an angry lion, fangs descending toward the mounds of pillows below. The walls were draped with colorful rugs of reds, oranges, and yellows.

Micah moved across the strange room to its single window. He peered through, his vision obscured by bars on the outside with enormous vines swirling around them. Wherever this was, he was a prisoner.

The view outside the window was unimaginable. A forest extended beyond the skyline, plush with deep green undergrowth. *I must be dreaming,* he thought. He couldn't take his eyes from the spellbinding beauty outside the window.

A loud, thudding knock sounded on the double wooden doors of the room. The door slid quietly open, and a small girl dressed in a white gown appeared. She could have been no more than ten years of age, with pale skin like satin and eyes of pale, creamy blue. She looked like a ghost, although an unusually cute one.

In a polite, soft voice, she said, "Excuse me, Mr. Purifier, sir; I have brought you a change of cloaks. Lord Raptor will see you now."

She attempted a smile and made a small curtsy. To Micah, she looked frightened; in fact, he could feel her fear. Although he could not completely believe that his situation was real, he gave the girl a welcoming smile.

"You can call me Micah. Tell me, dear, what is your name?" He could hardly believe the sound of his own voice—his tongue seemed to have picked up the accent of someone of Celtic descent.

"My name is Brianna, sir. I am known as Miss Brie. Drinks will be served as you enter the dining hall, which is down the stairs to the right." She curtsied again and left the room, closing the doors behind her.

This place was as real as the prick of a needle on the tip of one's finger. Micah supposed that Lord Raptor was the thing that brought him here. The evil name sounded vaguely familiar—as though he had read it in a book a long time ago. He looked at the dark, bulky cloak Brianna had dropped on the floor of his chamber. His own garments were tattered and bloodied from the car crash. He wondered if this was what happened after death, but swallowed the thought and threw the cloak over his own clothes. He found a belt with a silver seal for a buckle and used it to fasten the robe. The Converse shoes he wore to Sandy's house were still on his feet.

Everything in the room, from the furniture to the cloak he slipped on, appeared to be of the finest quality—luxury goods manufactured in the fashion of five hundred years ago. Perhaps he would have a chance to use the elegant bathtub if he had to stay here for a while.

He strode down the long corridor outside his room, noting the menacing statues posted at intervals along the walls. As he paced down the black marble hallway to the stairs, his footsteps echoed behind him like a never-ending percussion, fading away in the distance stride by stride. The stairs were wide and few, and as Micah came to the bottom of them, he saw a table set up beneath a marvelous chandelier of ancient crystals which sent out dazzling sparkles of light. The dark shadow of a man sat waiting for him.

"If it is not Sir Michael, the Purifier. What a…pleasure…it is for me to see you in my presence once again," he said in a horrible, unbelievably low tone.

"You must be Lord Raptor," Micah replied without a flinch.

"Ah, that I am. I would appreciate it if you would pronounce it 'Rapt'oor.' I hope Miss Brie was swift and polite."

"What do you want with me, or her? What the fuck is this shit?" Micah demanded.

"Miss Brie, bring the Purifier a glass of my finest brandy. You do still drink, don't you, sir?" Lord Raptor said, his smile revealing the glimmer of white fangs.

Micah didn't answer the question. Brianna rushed in, bearing a tray with two very fancy heavily cut glasses, and a matching decanter of an amber-colored liquor. She filled the glasses, placed one in front of Lord Raptor, and handed one to Micah. The girl stared at him as he sniffed the alcohol and then tossed it back in a swift, one-handed motion. He placed the glass on the table, and as the timid girl moved her hand to retrieve it, he caught her wrist and held it.

"Miss Brie, is this man keeping you hostage here?" Micah asked, his tone bold.

Brianna trembled, and a shadow passed over her eyes. She shivered in his grasp and pulled away, disappearing beyond a curtain at the side of the table.

Lord Raptor laughed. "Miss Brie is not my hostage, Sir Micah. She is my prisoner, one of many prisoners I keep here in the Temple of Purgatory—in case you are wondering where you sit."

He chuckled, downed his glass of liquor, and poured himself another. He slid the decanter across the table to Micah, who refilled his glass. At least Lord Raptor had good booze.

The effects of the alcohol began to warm Micah, and he stared in silence across the table. They sat for several moments before Lord Raptor slowly rose and made his way toward Micah. He was tall and evil looking with his glowing eyes and cruel, snarling grin. He gazed down at Micah, whose skin began to crawl with goose bumps as the creature kept his eyes locked on him. Micah stared down at the table, refusing to meet the creature's eyes. From the corner of his right eye, he could see Lord Raptor's long, green, pointed fingers swirling on the rim of the glass he had brought with him. The silence seemed to go on for years as he waited for Lord Raptor to speak.

Micah's face became hot, and to break the evil spell, he reached for the decanter of brandy. Lord Raptor reached for it at the same time, and there was a disturbing awkwardness as they moved in sync. Micah felt a small jolt and removed his arm from the table. Lord Raptor did not flinch. He gave a bone-chilling guffaw and filled both glasses. "Jumpy, are we?"

"What do you want with me?" Micah asked.

He forced himself to look up at his captor, which turned out to be another bad idea. The demon's face was large and terrifying. His features were somewhat human, though his greenish skin was stretched over his skull like a reptile's. His yellow eyes were merciless, and now that Micah was caught in the creature's glare, he knew that somehow he recognized him.

"Don't play stupid with me, Sir Micah. It's been a thousand years since our last encounter."

Lord Raptor shot out his arm and clasped Micah's neck in his claws. Micah instinctively wrapped his own hands around the demon's arm, petrified with fear. The creature held tight and spoke in a snakelike whisper.

"You are the Purifier, and I am Lord Raptor, keeper of the Temple of Purgatory. You, sir, have known this since the beginning of time. This will be my only humbling, Sir Micah. I have served you drink and offered politeness. I think that I have been more than cordial to you. Why must you break the rules of my Temple? If there is another occurrence of your purifications, I will not be so nice. Take your worthless existence back to your sorry room and slink away like you should. I will always win. Remember that. Do not make me squeeze the souls of the people you love with these same hands."

KELLY AND TAYLOR

When Micah regained consciousness, he found himself lying in a hospital bed. Sandy and Robby were at his side. His bandaged head throbbed. Despite his blurry vision, he quickly recognized his surroundings. The car accident and the visit with the demon brought a profound clarity to him. There was no more question of his purpose. Micah was the Purifier—a prophet and messenger of God—and his task was just beginning.

"You're awake!" Robby said, followed by a slight cough.

"Michael! Oh, my God!" Sandy exclaimed and then called the nurse.

It was not that Micah felt ungrateful for their love, but he had something very important to do. He sat up in bed, swung his legs down, and ripped the IV's from his arms and the heart monitor from his chest. The pain in his head seemed to subside immediately. He walked from the bed toward the door. He felt Sandy's hands circle his waist in a weak attempt to stop him. He swiveled on his feet to face her, pulled her close, and kissed her mouth with his eyes closed. He didn't give her the satisfaction of seeing him

50

wait for her full reaction. He strode into the hallway, ignoring the voices of the nurses behind the service desk, and made his way to the elevator.

Entering the elevator, he punched the ground floor button. Exiting, he walked down the hallway toward the emergency room, where there was a lot of commotion. As he entered emergency cubicle 16-C, he caught an older woman in his arms as she fainted and fell backward. Two nurses, who had been behind him in the hallway, now dropped to their knees so Micah could place the woman's head in their hands. He stepped over her and entered the room.

Before him, a family stood around the bed of a young girl. He already knew that her name was Kelly, and that she had just been pronounced dead. The doctors were trying to hold back her brother, father, and grandmother. Micah assumed that the woman he caught was the mother. Kelly's hospital dressings were bloody, and her heart monitor—still flat-lining—was unattended. Kelly's spirit huddled in the corner of the room crying.

She and her boyfriend, Taylor, were riding his motorcycle—having fun, but going too fast. Taylor cut a corner and ran head on into an oncoming car. Taylor lay in the room next to Kelly, both legs broken. Though still alive, he could not contact Kelly or see her. Michael knew that while Taylor's body was trapped in a dreamless, drug-induced sleep, his heart was desperate for Kelly.

The doctors saw Micah come in, and silence descended on the crowd around the bed. An angelic ambiance thickened the energy of the room as Micah knelt down next to Kelly's spirit and placed his hand on her shoulder. She peered out from beneath the arm that covered her face. He could, in that moment, feel and know every part of her past. She had lived for twenty-six years, and everyone who knew her loved her. She was an angel, but although she no longer felt any physical pain, her soul would remain in pain and sadness for many years to follow unless he could purify her. This girl, so beautiful with her blue eyes and auburn hair, was confused and terribly frightened. All she could do was cry.

"I am Sir Micah, the Purifier. You are OK, Kelly. Now, tell your family what you want to tell them so we can get this part over with. Then I will give you to your boyfriend. He's waiting for you."

Kelly stared at Micah in astonishment and then stood up without questioning him.

"Mom," Kelly said.

She looked around the room in hope. Her brother gasped as Kelly's voice rang out, loud and clear, seeming to come from every angle of the room. In that moment, there was no world outside of emergency unit 16-C. It was ironic that life could be felt so strongly in an hour of complete loss.

Kelly's mother did not hesitate. She came through the door where she had fallen.

"Kelly? Sweetheart? Where are you?"

She looked around and began to move slowly toward the bed, where her dead daughter was hidden beneath a blanket.

"I'm over here, Mom! In the corner. This man is helping me talk to you," Kelly said as she began to cry again.

Micah kept his head down and his hand still on Kelly's shoulder.

"Mom, Dad, Matthew, Grandma, I'm OK. I'm dead, but I...I'm OK."

"Kelly! My baby!" cried her mother.

"Kelly!" both her brother and father cried out.

They scrambled to the floor at Micah's and Kelly's feet, weeping. Her brother bowed his head in prayer.

"I love you all," Kelly said. "Don't worry about me. I'm still here."

"I want to see you, Kelly," her mother said, weeping. She rested her head in her hands, shoulders slumped in despair.

Kelly looked at Micah with an impossible question in her eyes, but he was not worried. He reached out with his left arm, cupped her mother's chin, and raised it from her hands.

"Look upon her…all of you. This will be the last time," Micah boomed in a loud, deep, and reverent tone.

They all lifted their heads in hope and saw Kelly's pretty earthly form coalesce in the corner of the room, the white walls behind her. She smiled with a face drenched in tears. Her family knew she was at peace.

Kelly's family departed the hospital, leaving the stunned doctors behind them. Micah left Kelly to give her love and warmth to Taylor in the next room. The hospital seemed to be noticeably peaceful, at least for the time being. The halls were quiet and the vibes calm.

Kelly lay with her body over Taylor's, tears of joy streaming down her face. He was cold, and she warmed him. Michael knew that she would always savor the memory of this special moment. She fell asleep, blending herself into his dream of seeing her once again.

JEREMY

The water of the lake lay calm for Jeremy. It had been years since he went fishing. He and his young son had often fished this lake, but Jeremy hadn't done much of anything in the three years since his wife passed away. He didn't really know quite why he decided to come today, but he didn't regret it. He knew he would have to fish by himself, but his old house had become so lonely that this day on the lake felt uplifting.

Jeremy was quiet and at peace with the world around him as he listened to the water below softly lapping a rhythm against the old aluminum of the twelve-foot bass floater. Every so often, the tiniest drop of water would pop up from a ripple against the side. There were no other people on the lake today. He remembered years ago when the happy screams of children playing on the shore would echo through the breeze during the summer, along with the occasional manly ruckus coming from other fishermen in boats on the lake. If only he had known then how much he would miss those sounds now. He missed hoping that his boy would catch a huge fish, and he missed the way that he would look up at him when he did catch one. His son hoped that his daddy would be proud of him, holding up that poor old catfish, and he had been. Jeremy had been so proud.

He looked up at the sky and then at the trees around the solemn lake, haunted by happy memories. He smiled to himself and reeled in his line. As he hooked another worm, he could see that his fingers were thin with age, knobbed and wrinkled. He had almost not been able to finish the fisherman's knot he used to tie the hook. The water was calm, and he could see a family of ducks paddling, feet invisible under the water. The littlest one made funny little noises, as if it were in a hurry. The sun felt warm on Jeremy's skin, and at that moment he knew that he loved everything, even if there wouldn't be any fish today.

Jeremy was afraid to die.

ZELIUS

As there are demons, there are also angels who walk the earth to lay their blessings and live inside the skin of certain individuals in mystic secrecy. Every one of us has an angel or angels who watch over our spirits and our secrets. Zelius was Micah's Guardian Angel.

Zelius loved his Micah. He had watched over him since the birth of Micah's soul. From a boy to a youth to a man, Zelius guarded Micah. He had done his best to let Micah live and learn on his own, but he was always there when his charge needed him most. He would be there to embrace Micah in his arms and comfort him when he was finally through with his journey on earth. Until then, Zelius was there to watch and smile.

There were also things that could not be determined ahead of time. Zelius knew this, and he knew that there would be occasions when he would have to intervene in the spiritual realm. He also knew, and had always known, that Micah was a Purifier. What he hadn't been able to foresee was the danger now threatening his beloved Micah. He supposed that he should have been expecting this ever since the Almighty God gave him the task of watching over Micah. But the peril his charge now faced went far beyond a simple death. Micah was a very important soul in the universe, and although his enemy, Lord Raptor, was a lowly demon, he possessed the power to extinguish Micah's gift as a Purifier. Each time Micah reappeared in a new life, he was able to help other souls. If this gift were taken away, he would no longer be allowed to exercise his power to send people to the Forest of Beauty and they would languish in the Temple of Purgatory.

The Angel Knight Sir Zelius could not let this happen. He would risk his own life spirit to save that of his beloved Micah.

Damn Lord Raptor!

Zelius had never been an earthly Purifier, but he had battled with Lord Raptor for many millennia as the demon tried to use his wicked power to trap souls that did not belong in the Temple of Purgatory.

As an Angel Knight—not yet an Archangel, the highest rank in the immediate realm of the Almighty God—he held his position as honorably as he could and hoped that in time he would be picked to guard the throne of the Lord. He didn't care how many years it would take; in fact, he didn't know if he would make this dream come true. Still, he would strive to make it happen.

Now the time had come for Zelius to fend off evil once again. He was ready. Perhaps he would gain higher respect from the Almighty as long as he did his best. Even if he did not, Zelius hated Lord Raptor. The demon had sneaked into Micah's life like a cancer, and his evil work had not gone unnoticed.

Zelius sat on one of the great branches of a tree in the Forest of Beauty. Their tops resembled an endless mesa of clouds, except that they were green. As he moved his hazel eyes over the foliage, he could see the towers of the Temple of Purgatory rising in the distance like horrible black spikes. It appeared as though the Temple was trying to conceal itself in the forest like an alligator beneath the water waiting to catch its prey. He reminded himself that there was a purpose for the Temple, even if it was currently governed by a demon.

Before Lord Raptor had turned the Temple into an evil place by making his home there, the Temple of Purgatory had been a place for souls to find themselves and eventually be released. They would either be purified and move on to Heaven, or, if they found faults in everyone but themselves, they would be cast into the dark places.

Lord Raptor did not own the Temple; he just thought he did. Long ago, Zelius had heard, Lord Raptor was an Angel Knight himself, sent to the temple to guard the souls and reside with them there. It was a wonderful honor and gift to Lord Raptor from the Almighty. But Lord Raptor became stupid and greedy with his new power and turned away from the Almighty God. He hid away from the Temple, frightening the new souls who were already lost in their consciousness, and he did it all with an evil smile upon his face. Over the years, his skin became green, and his teeth became sharp. Slowly but surely, the features of his once-comely face became hideous.

Zelius slipped from the branch to the soft, moist floor of the forest, a half-mile drop he made landing lightly on his feet. As an angel, he could do such things. The fluffy white wolves of the forest appeared from the surrounding trunks and bushes to patter silently toward him. The wolves loved Zelius and took small, gleeful leaps around his feet. On any other day, he would have played and wrestled with them and then fallen asleep with them in the warm sunlight, embracing them as if he were a wolf himself.

Today, however, Zelius needed to regain his dexterity and test his agility. Soon he would battle once again. He held his strong arms before himself. At eight feet tall, Zelius wore a glorious white satin cloak that skimmed just above his knees and swirled around his elbows. A golden belt wrapped tightly around his trim waist bore a sheath and a sword with a magnificent blade extending three feet in length. He grasped the hilt, which was adorned with shining jewels, and held the sword to the sky, catching the sparkling rays of sun poking through the dense forest.

The wolves lifted their heads at his motion, spellbound at the sight of the heavenly Zelius, his golden hair falling around his broad shoulders in curls, his dazzling sword cutting through the streaks of sunlight that glinted off the metal. He was, indeed, an angelic sight.

CHURCH OF THE PEOPLE

Movie Buff had been closed for a week. Sandy pleaded with Micah to stay at home while she took care of the place, but he resisted, insisting that Sandy remain at home to watch Robby. The boy was sick again, and Micah knew their grandmother needed help.

As Micah's power increased, he began to feel the presence of spirits who needed him many times each day. The family to whom he had given his aid at the hospital somehow found out his name and telephone number. They called a dozen times, leaving messages of praise on his answering machine.

He had, in the past, been a private person. Although he was beginning to enjoy the acknowledgment from the people he helped, he had recently acquired a daily habit of picking up a half-pint of fine tequila from Henry's Liquor. Everything that was happening was quite overwhelming, and he was drinking throughout the day to calm his nerves.

On Friday, Micah went by Movie Buff to check on things. It had been a long week. He and Sandy would go back to work on

Monday. The regular Movie Buff customers might have been confused as to why the place had simply been locked up and unattended for days, so he thought he would stop by and place a sign in the window stating when it would be open again. He stopped by Henry's Liquor to purchase his usual. It was only nine o'clock in the morning when he strode in, wearing a long black overcoat that caught the wind at his waist. It was now the middle of October, and the Arizona air was chilling.

Sing looked up, as he always did when anyone entered his store. He sat on a chair behind the counter reading his paper, his face showing a light hint of concern.

"Why so early this morning, Micah?" he asked, eyes peering over the top of his bifocals.

"I'll take the regular, Sing—a small bottle of Patrón."

Micah took the bottle from the counter, replacing it with a twenty-dollar bill. He pulled his special silver flask—it had been his father's—from his coat pocket and poured the contents in. He set the empty bottle back on the counter, took a swig from the flask, and winked at Sing without answering his question. He stepped outside and lit a cigarette after taking two more sips of the tequila. As he fastened the top of the flask, he could feel the burn in his stomach. He loved it. It was as though his blood absorbed the alcohol like a sponge, and he could feel it running through his veins.

It seemed as though the streets of the town were always deserted. As he walked the sidewalks, he was puzzled at how so much trash could accumulate in the gutters without people to leave it there. The day was gloomy and overcast, and he could not see much of the sun behind the gray sky.

The Church of the People was located two blocks west of Micah's apartment. It shone with fresh white paint, and a steeple topped with a simple wooden cross rose from the center of its roof. It was surrounded by trees, neatly trimmed bushes, and a family park. He had never been to the pretty little church before. He paused before entering through the tall white doors to down another large gulp from his flask. He closed his eyes for a moment, head lifted toward the sky, and then stumbled inside.

The interior appeared larger than it seemed from the outside. No service was in progress, and the only other visitor was a figure in white sitting near the right wall. Whoever he was, he was extremely tall, with golden curls flowing down his shoulders. The man seemed to be in deep prayer, for he did not raise his bowed head when Micah entered. Micah respectfully ignored him and made his way down the center aisle between rows of wooden pews. He had forgotten how much he liked the feeling of a church; it felt safe inside. He inhaled the sweet smell of the freshly polished old pine-wood benches, and felt the soft warmth of flickering candles lazily melting below a beautiful sculpture of Jesus Christ on the cross.

Micah slipped into an empty pew and bowed his head. He had not prayed in many years and wasn't sure how to do so now, but he decided it didn't matter. God would understand.

"Lord, Heavenly Father. I bow before you today to remind myself and you, Heavenly Father, of my love for you and your Son. I have come to extreme events in my life on earth, dear Heavenly Father. Please help guide me through these trials. Please take care of my beloved father who lives with you now, for I miss him so much. Please help little Robby get well, because he is very sick. Amen."

His body began to sway from side to side. Tears, induced both by the tequila and by thoughts of his deceased father, ran down his cheeks. He stayed in place for a moment of silence and then rose and turned to walk out. As Micah passed down the center aisle, Zelius watched him and smiled.

THE CHALLENGE

Outside the church, Micah continued to drink. He was now no longer concerned with making it to Movie Buff and decided to explore the lovely little park behind the church.

When he prayed inside, he felt closer to his father, and that closeness made him want to linger around the church. He thought he would come here more often. He staggered in zigzags through the grass toward the shade of the trees, away from the little playground where he saw a mother and her toddler playing in the sandbox. The sun was high, and the breeze was peaceful. He moved under a tree whose branches hung low over the ground, littering the soil with its leaves, and let his overcoat fall on top of them. Micah could barely stand upright as he attempted to unscrew the flask for another drink.

As he bent his head to look more closely at the troublesome lid, a very large white hand reached toward the sternum of his chest and pushed. Micah collapsed onto his back, confused but—thanks to his alcohol-dulled reactions—hardly startled. He stared up at the enormous man draped in bright white clothing. The sun behind him seemed to radiate off the rich curls of golden blond hair that circled his strong-chinned face. He stood still, smiling.

"Look at you, dear Micah. Drunk from strong wine and living like a bum at a family park. Beg your Almighty to forgive you," said the man in a loud, bold voice.

"Who the fuck are you?" Micah demanded.

The man chuckled. "Dear, dear Micah, I am your Guardian Angel, Zelius of the Welken, and I have come to intervene."

"Intervene? Spare me."

Micah brought the flask to his lips, only to have it kicked from his hand before he could take a drink.

"Ouch! Man, what the fuck!"

He tried to rise to his feet, pushing himself up on his arms, swaying and unbalanced. The man pushed him over again with a foot to Micah's shoulder.

"You are going to get sober, and you are going to be physically fit for what is ahead of you. I will see to it," Zelius said without the slightest bit of humor in his booming voice. He no longer smiled.

"Listen, uh, Zelius. I've had a long week. I'd really just like to be left alone, so..."

Zelius bent forward and clutched Micah's collar, pulling him to his feet before Micah could finish his sentence. He was suddenly on his feet, and the violent motion made him purge. He vomited on the ground, the bitter tequila spurting from his nostrils and mouth.

"How are you supposed to defend yourself from the violence that Lord Raptor will bring to you if you are weak from strong wine, Micah?"

Zelius cupped Micah's face in his hands and forced him to meet his eyes.

"I have come to teach you how to become a basic warrior, at the least. I will try to protect you the best I can, but the time may come when you have to save your own life—and the lives of others, as well."

Zelius looked sincere and loving as Micah leaned on him. His appearance had a sobering effect, and Micah pulled away, trying to straighten himself. He knew Zelius was telling the truth, considering the other events that had taken place in the last few days.

He breathed a long sigh. "Can I have a couple of days to consider?" he asked, giving up on his resistance.

"There is no other option to consider. We will start tomorrow morning. I will arrive early at your home," Zelius said.

"Oh great! You know where I live, too?"

Zelius didn't answer the question. "Time is crucial, Micah. You will need your sleep."

"What's the rush? I just became the Purifier."

"Your soul has had the power to purify the spirits of others since the beginning of humankind. Lord Raptor has not been around nearly as long as you. You will remember soon. But until then, you must know that Lord Raptor and his forces of evil plan to stop you. First, he will capture the boy, Robby; then your Sandy; and then you. He wishes to cut you down, one by one. He will eventually cast your father into the realm of darkness unless you defend against him. I will help you, Micah. We must fight together, for Lord Raptor has grown very powerful."

Zelius was both motivating and uncompromising. Micah once again felt the anger rise within him. His emotions were no longer dulled by drunkenness.

"Tomorrow," he said.

"Good heavens, Micah. It is good to know you are back. This earth needs you now more than ever before."

With that he soared into the sky like a bird with no wings, spreading his arms wide from his shoulders, resembling the crucifix inside the church.

Micah watched him as he disappeared into the sky. As his gaze returned to earth, he saw that the pretty mother and child in the sandbox sat looking up at him with mouths agape. He smiled at them nonchalantly and drifted over to the spot where he had ditched his special flask. He picked it up and started home.

SAMUEL AND MICAH

Samuel, too, had been thinking about the accident in front of Movie Buff. He was the first officer called to the scene of the tragic crash and had immediately noticed the man talking to the car's driver, seeming to glow with a supernatural force.

Samuel had never particularly believed in paranormal activity, but he was at the end of his rope. He could not sleep at night after losing Chad. He knew that he had contributed to his son's depression and crimes and, at the end, to his violent suicide. He had not seen his wife in over two years now, and he had no one with whom to share his grief. The memories of his son caused him excruciating emotional pain, but that was not the only thing keeping him awake at night.

He often left his dirty dishes and trash out on the kitchen counters. He remembered when he washed the dishes or cleaned up after himself, because it didn't happen often. He went to bed, ate, tried to sleep, woke up, ate again, and arrived at work early.

Night terrors and infinite sadness brought Samuel to a state of numbness. He took pride in nothing but his work, where he kept himself so occupied that he was able to keep the thought of his dead son out of his mind—at least to a slight degree. Chad had been dead for two months now.

About a month back, Samuel headed off for work and left his home—his old home, the one with so many memories—in its usual state of filth. It had been over a week since he had cleaned anything. The counter above the trash can was cluttered with empty TV dinner trays. Dishes and pans, with the remains of cooked eggs and waffle batter stuck to them were piled on the sink counter. He arrived home that night to find everything in place, and spotless. He called out to his ex-wife and searched for a note, but there was none. The dishes were put away in their cabinets, washed and dried. The three trash bags were closed and tied, heaped in a corner.

Samuel felt a presence that could not be mistaken for anything else in the world. He stood, unable to move, listening to a door slam in a room he had barely stepped into in the last four years— Chad's room. Samuel felt a chill move up his back. He forced himself to walk from the kitchen and ascend the stairs with a careful pace. He could hear more ruckus as he reached the floor that Chad had once occupied. He knew there was no worldly intruder; his son was there. Samuel opened the door and gasped. There, alert and watching, Chad sat in the empty corner that had once held his bed. Samuel clutched at the door frame and fell to his knees.

"Why did you throw me away?" cried Chad's apparition.

"No, son. No…oh God, I would never!"

Chad seemed not to hear his father.

"My bed! My desk! Everything! Even me!"

"Oh, son, I…"

Samuel watched his son's beautiful ghostly form disappear into the cobwebbed shadows of his abandoned room. He was gone. Samuel called and called for his son to reappear. He could not believe that he had seen Chad's spirit. There was no more of him.

For days and days following the event, Samuel longed to see his son. He thought that Chad would have wanted to stay to listen to his father speak of his sorrows but was afraid that his son had not been able to hear him speak at all. The very idea that Chad had seen him and not been able to hear or finish what he had to say burned into Samuel as much as the guilt of not trying harder to find him when he had been in need. Chad did not come again, at least not that Samuel was aware of.

He knew that he had to find a way to get in touch with his son, and he had an idea that the man who spoke to the dying individual at the car crash might have the knowledge he needed.

Chad's ghost continued to reach out from his spiritual realm, although only when Samuel was at work. Samuel regularly left unwashed dishes on the sink counter knowing that every time, without fail, he would arrive home to find them washed, dried, and put away in the cupboard where they belonged.

He thought he remembered the man at the crash scene from the video store; he had rented a movie there one time. He also recalled smelling alcohol on the man's breath. It had been a while, but Samuel thought about having a drink or two himself.

He drove to town toward Movie Buff, hoping to find the man. The day was not yet over, and he thought perhaps he might catch him closing up his shop.

The day seemed strange to Samuel. There were hardly any clouds of significance, yet it was overcast. Usually, on Fridays, the streets of this small Arizona town were occupied by dating couples and dog walkers out enjoying the early evening. This day, however, seemed different. Samuel would be damned if he could spot one lonely car besides his own, and there was not another person in sight.

He breathed a sigh of relief when he saw a dark-haired man in a thick black coat standing at the door of Movie Buff, obviously locking up just as he had anticipated. As Samuel pulled the police car up to the curb, the man raised a silver flask to his lips.

Perfect! thought Samuel.

He flashed his lights and buzzed his siren a single time, a quick *errk.*

"Oh shit!" mumbled Micah under his breath. He swung around, flask still in hand, as the cop stepped out of the car.

"Havin' a little sip, are we?"

Busted!

"Please turn around, sir, arms up, legs spread," Samuel said.

Micah did as asked, cursing under his rank-smelling breath.

Samuel patted him down and then spun him around. Micah moved willingly.

"Look, Officer…" Micah began, but the policeman cut him off.

Samuel didn't beat around the bush. He looked Micah straight in the eyes. "That was you at that car accident a couple of weeks ago, wasn't it?" he asked.

Micah immediately felt an uneasy pressure. Could the cop possibly have known what his purpose for being there really was? He considered telling him that he was merely trying to help because he worked at Movie Buff, but he had arrived at the scene too late. Would this cop know? He realized that he was still standing there looking dumbly at the cop, drunk and not answering his questions. Before he could respond, the cop spoke again.

"I know it was you. You spoke to the man before he died. Whatever you were doing, the feeling was…indescribable. I need your help."

Micah stared at the policeman in bewilderment.

"Well, I suppose I could arrest you for being drunk in public," Samuel offered with a smile.

Micah relaxed a little. "I'm sure that won't be necessary," he replied. He held out his hand to shake.

"Samuel," the cop said and clasped Micah's hand in a firm grip.

"Michael Joseph, but you can call me Micah."

Samuel asked, "Where can we talk? You got a car?"

"I do, but not with me. Maybe you could give me a ride to my house—that is, if I don't have to wear cuffs."

UNEXPECTED LOVE

As Sandy studied her reflection in the bathroom mirror, she felt redefined. She had not had many boyfriends in her life up to that point. Yes, of course, she had been in love back in her high school years, but between that period of time and now, she had not felt a rush quite like the one she was experiencing at the moment.

Her mother had been gone for a long while, and she continually mourned her loss. She tried to keep her emotions held in as best she could, but sometimes it was hard not to succumb to her grief. It had already been seven years since her graduation from high school. The death of her mother and now the illness of the little brother she loved so dearly made it seem as if time were passing impossibly fast.

Sandy and her brother loved movies. Because they had experienced so much grief and turmoil together, watching all kinds of movies as an escape from their problems was a favorite activity of theirs. She knew she should not be letting Rob watch R-rated movies at his age, but she did anyway. Besides, Robby himself knew and introduced his big sister to many new titles that were rated R. Over the last couple of years they enjoyed staying up late on the weekends to watch new movies together, giggling at their grandmother's ongoing commentary about the "rubbish" they watched---until she drank herself into a heavy snoring sleep in her chair.

Watching movies together was a way for them to block out the reality of Robby's pneumonia flare-ups and the sad loss of their parents. There wasn't much else to do in the small town where they lived. When Sandy got her job at Movie Buff, she gained access to many more titles, and Micah was so cool he would let her borrow as many as she wanted. In fact, over the last few months Sandy had pretty much become the only person who worked there. Except for the times when Micah came in to check on things and lock up the place or open the store, Movie Buff felt like hers alone.

And then there was Micah himself. She couldn't stop from blushing when she thought about him. She knew he had a drinking problem—he was a handsome, kind man with a drinking problem. He was so sexy, though! As she looked at herself in the mirror, she felt that rush again.

She had forgotten how pretty she was. Now what was she going to do? She realized that she had barely been putting any makeup on to go to work; Micah had seen her just the way she was, for months. She didn't like how freckled her cheeks were or the way her hair was combed, just hanging. She hadn't felt like this in so long.

"Oh, no you can't," Sandy said to herself. "He's your boss! Oh, the hell with it."

She opened the medicine cabinet for no reason, gave it a light push shut, and then wandered into the living room.

How happy she felt today. Robby was OK, even though he had been ordered to stay in the hospital for an extra night so his doctor could monitor his coughing. He was hacking so hard that they had to keep him on an IV. Sandy always felt more comfortable when Robby had medical attention.

This feeling of safety allowed her to relax and ponder her personal life. Micah was so dreamy. He had just pulled the IVs out of his strong arms and walked out of the room. But not until after he pulled her close and brushed her lips with his.

The fact that Micah could connect with the spirits of the dead was extraordinary, although it was no surprise to Sandy. She knew that he had performed an amazing act the other night at the hospital, although she didn't witness it herself.

The incident was covered in the next day's newspaper, and Sandy read the story three times. She wondered if Micah knew that his name was in the paper. The headline read: "Grieving family claims that local man reunited them with deceased daughter while in the hospital." *What an amazing man he is,* thought Sandy. He reminded her of the superheroes in the movies she and Robby watched. Micah was real, though, and so was all of this—whatever "this" was.

Sandy puttered around her little kitchen, adjusting this and that, not really doing anything particularly important. She didn't want to go to sleep quite yet. She decided she would open a new bottle of the kind of wine she had shared with Micah. If he liked it so much, she would buy more bottles. He was so nice. The wine was the only sort of alcohol Sandy kept in the house—besides her grandmother's brandy, which she didn't think would have been appropriate to offer. Now she wondered if he would have preferred it. Either way, Micah was accepting of everything he had found in her house: the wine, her sleeping grandmother, and her sickly little brother. He was also really charming and kind to Robby.

Sandy was mature enough not to be embarrassed about her family and the possible differences between her home and those of other people, but she was grateful for Micah's acceptance and warmth.

She poured herself a glass of the wine. Even though she wasn't much of a drinker and didn't particularly love the taste of wine, it did make her throat warm. She held the bottle up and looked at it. She read the label aloud—"mer-lot?"—wondering if she was pronouncing it correctly. The store called it "Two Buck Chuck" and the clerk told her it was a really good buy for the money! Sandy thought it looked like a good bottle, and since it only cost her a couple of dollars she could buy more! She wondered if Micah really liked it, or if he had just told her that to make her feel good. Either way, it made her giggle as the wine trickled down into her belly. She didn't notice that she was smiling, or that her grandmother was awake in her chair watching her.

"Must be a new man," her grandmother said.

"Gram! No! I was just..."

"Aw shucks, honey, I know that look anywhere, and you look as giddy as you did back in grade school," Grandma said with a warm smile.

"OK. Hey, I didn't know you were awake."

"Be a dear and fix me some coffee, would you?" her grandmother asked. "How is Robby?"

"He's good for now. I'm hoping to pick him up tomorrow."

She brewed a pot of coffee, enough for both of them, and her grandmother sat at the little table with Sandy and listened. Sandy told her about her new relationship with her boss. It was nice to sit down with her grandmother, whom she loved very much, and just talk over a cup of coffee. Sandy realized, suddenly, that it had been a long time since they had done this.

She and Grandma had never had a cross word between them for as long as she could remember, despite the tough times. But lately they hadn't talked much for different reasons. Sandy didn't care what those reasons were. They were a small family and needed to sit down and have coffee together more often, even if that was the only thing they could find time to do together.

Finally, Sandy brought herself to ask the question that had been on her mind the whole time they had been talking: "Gram... will you stop drinking so much?"

"Well dear, I know I should. I have used the brandy as a crutch for too long. I'm sorry Sandy. I started drinking to escape the sadness after your mother died. I will try harder. You know it feels so good to talk to you as an adult now. I love you and Robby so very much. I promise you I will stop."

Sandy and Grandma shared a nice hour together that night.

Love can truly change the tide.

SÉANCE

Micah and Samuel sat on opposite sides of the glass coffee table in front of Micah's couch. The curtains were closed, even though the sun was setting and hardly any remaining light peeked through. Micah placed small tea-light candles in cylindrical glass holders throughout the room. They were left over from his candlelight evenings with Janine. She always insisted that candles gave a romantic ambience to their evenings together.

Micah showed no reluctance to assist Samuel in contacting his son. As they drove to Micah's apartment, he listened to Samuel closely, seemingly intrigued by the story of Chad's tragic ending and the incidents that followed. He interrupted only to ask Samuel to stop by a strange little shop called the Mystic Temple, one that Samuel didn't recall seeing before. Micah picked up a small bundle of some incense. He also asked him to swing by Henry's Liquor for a few necessary items.

Watching Micah emerge with his brown paper sack, Samuel was struck by the foolishness of hoping for prophesy from this drunken man. He thought that calling the whole thing off might be a wise idea, and was about to say so, when they reached Micah's apartment.

Now, sitting quietly across the table from Micah and watching the swift and confident way he moved around the room, Samuel swallowed in nervous disbelief of his previous thoughts. The room had grown quite dark; the tiny flames of the candles swayed and danced on their wicks, casting shadows upon Micah's drawn face and carving dark hollows and caverns around the bones of his cheek and jaw.

The two men exchanged no more than a handful of words, but Samuel felt an increasing sense of liking for Micah as he watched him bustle about, so eager to help a stranger.

The neck of a Patrón tequila bottle clinked on the edge of one glass and then a second that Samuel guessed was for him, breaking the silence in the room. It had been rough with the drink lately, and Samuel was trying to cut back, but he was not about to deny himself this fine liquor—not at this moment. Micah set the short, fat glass bottle to the side of the two full shot glasses, picked them up, and handed one across the table to Samuel, who accepted it politely. As he reached for the glass, he could feel the candle's warmth on the bottom of his arm. He didn't know what to expect next, but the feeling was exciting.

Micah raised his glass and said, "To the dead."

"Yes, and to my son."

They tapped the shots together, brought them to their lips, and let the burning liquid fall down their throats.

The scent of the alcohol lingered on Samuel's tongue and the reek of the incense sticks filled his nostrils, creating a powerful smell. He leaned his back against the couch cushions and watched as Micah did the same in his chair, leaning so far back that his eyes appeared as white globes.

A bright light filled the room, and Samuel felt his earthly consciousness expand like the beginning of a wondrous dream. He felt as though his vision was drifting and free, soaring like a bird in the sky. He realized that he was lying on his back, cushioned softly in cool moss. He peered up and saw beautiful trees, brushing against each other. He rested there for a moment, the quiet broken only by the light friction of their leaves. He did not care what time it was, what day it was, where he was. The sunlight streaked through the sea of green surrounding him. It was not bright enough to bother his eyelids as he shut them again, savoring this pleasure.

I could lie here forever, thought Samuel. Then he heard Micah's voice above him.

"OK, Samuel. You can wake up now. We're here."

Samuel opened his eyes and saw Micah's smiling face looking down at him, hair dark against the sun behind him. He stared for a moment, still not positive about what was happening. Micah bent over slowly and offered his hand. Samuel grasped it, and Micah pulled him to his feet. They stood in a small meadow, near a pool of water surrounded by what seemed to be endless trees. Micah stood gazing at their surroundings like a small boy at an amusement park.

"This is the Forest of Beauty. Isn't it gorgeous?" Micah said.

Samuel studied him for a moment. A broad, bold smile lit Micah's usually solemn face. He looked truly happy. He no longer wore his thick, heavy trench coat but a simple robe of light brown, laced down the middle with a hefty dirk strapped to his side. He looked like a fourteenth-century peasant warrior. Micah smiled again and began walking toward the edge of the tree line.

"Hey...wait," Samuel protested.

Suddenly, he found himself thrown to his knees by an unseen—but very furry—force, his hands making imprints in the mud.

He screamed, "Help!"

His speech was muffled by a soft snout and strong tongue, pushing against Samuel's chin and mouth in a playful manner.

"What the hell!"

Samuel sat back, now eye to eye with a white dog of some sort. The dog's eyes were the pearl white of seashells, wide and happy. Micah was now by his side, crouched and petting the animal. As if on cue, two more appeared out of the brush.

"These are the white wolves of the Forest of Beauty. They won't hurt you. They're here for us to love and to help the ones in need," Micah said.

The wolf bobbed his snowy head to the motion of Micah's petting hand. Samuel stretched out his own arm to stroke the wolf's cheek. He remembered what it was like to feel the fluff of a dog's fur against the palm of his hand, and he missed these friendly moments with the companion he had given away so unthinkingly in his sadness and anger. He felt closer to the feared unknown than ever, but everything seemed to be so peaceful here in this magical place. Samuel was now fully aware and believing.

The wolf suddenly barked, sprang backward to land on his feet, and hunched down on his front paws in a playful pose. He swung his tail from side to side and moved his pointed head from Micah to Samuel and back again.

"It's time now. He'll show us the way," Micah said.

Samuel couldn't help but notice that all drunkenness and carelessness had completely left Micah's character. He was poised and certain, thoughtful and polite. He seemed—heroic.

On any other day, an experience such as this would have had Samuel ready to commit himself to an asylum. Today, he felt ready to gain knowledge outside of the world he knew. He had asked an extraordinary question, and Micah—the man to whom Samuel had come to when all else failed—was taking him in search of an extraordinary answer.

The white wolves led them through the towering trees and overgrowth of the forest. A creature in the trees above would have seen Micah, the wolves, and Samuel as small as insects among the giant roots where they walked. If there was any sunlight, it showed itself only by bringing out the colors of the plants and the burgundy color of the bark encasing the trees. The smell of damp wood and mud in the air seemed to cleanse their lungs with refreshing oxygen.

As Micah trailed the wolves, Samuel followed them cautiously. At times, his steps slowed enough that Micah called to him to keep up the pace. Samuel was an older man, and the way was full of obstacles formed by the rocks, vines, and bulging roots that humped themselves boldly out of the dark soil. Samuel had never seen any place like this in his life. He didn't have to question it in his mind because he felt more alive in the Forest of Beauty than he had ever felt anywhere else.

The sweat was dripping down their faces, and they had completely lost track of time, when the wolves began to growl in unison: a low, rumbling sound not of attack, but of warning—and, perhaps, a hint of fear.

BRIANNA

"This is it!" Micah said, whipping the dagger from its sheath and carefully making his way to an overhang of branches in front of the un-cleared path. He pulled away the vines and brush with his daggered hand and beckoned Samuel to advance. Samuel was speechless and out of breath as he stared up at the destination they had hiked so far to reach.

With the wolf between them, they gazed in awe at the destination ahead—the Temple of Purgatory. It was a castle of black stone with the green patina of age, interlaced with old vines between the cracks. A clearing circled the temple, and its towers rose above the trees to scrape the sky.

"Wait here," Micah said.

He crept quietly forward to the base of the Temple wall. The wolf sat silently at Samuel's side, graciously nodding acceptance of Samuel's petting as they watched Micah take action. He simply looked up the wall for a short moment and then leaped to take hold of the protruding stones that provided him a spot to begin his ascent.

Micah climbed the vertical wall as quickly as a spider. He climbed with grace, though there were places where he hoped not to slip; many of the stones were smooth and weathered from the unthinkable amount of time that had elapsed. He did not want to seem fearful, but when he glanced over his shoulder to the unfathomable drop to the ground below him, he almost lost his grip.

There were slits for windows along the temple, covered with bars that prevented any living thing from entering or escaping. Micah finally came to the window he was searching for, peering through its bars to see little Brianna sitting in a chair reading. Micah had never visited Brianna's room in all his memory, but he wasn't worried about that: he had somehow sensed where the room was located. He knew the place as well as his own—after all, he was The Purifier.

He held himself close to the window with his left arm and reached his right through the bars to knock three times on the windowpane beyond them. Brianna raised her delicate head from her book to see Micah's face at her window.

"Shhh!" Brianna said as she opened the window. "Lord Raptor is asleep in his study. Oh please, Sir Micah, do not bring trouble here. If I am caught associating with you, the Lord will surely send me to the dungeons!"

Brianna's dimples flashed as she talked. Her face was soft and fair, but terrified as she spoke to Micah.

"You should not worry, little one. I am here to save you. But first, you must assist me in my task. You must let me inside and guide me to the dungeon of Chad, the son of Samuel. Do you know the place?"

"Oh, Sir Micah, I am afraid I cannot! I would have to take the keys from Lord Raptor himself. He will surely catch me!" Brianna pleaded.

Tears welled up in her pretty eyes, and Micah saw her fear—but he also saw hope and longing.

"You can do this, Miss Brie. I am the Purifier, and I promise you I will not fail you," Micah demanded.

"OK...I...I'll do it. You must move fast. We haven't much time."

She shut the window in Micah's face abruptly and then re-opened it to add, "Meet me around the bottom in the front—the doors below the mount of crows."

Brianna shut the window again and scurried out of her bed-room. Micah immediately began to climb back down the tower to the ground below, where Samuel and the wolf were still waiting.

Brianna tiptoed through the halls she had come to know so well with the same gracefulness she had when alive. She died from cancer one year and one month previously, leaving behind a mother, father, and baby brother who all loved her dearly. Brianna had attended church every Sunday morning for as long as she could remember, and she had been permitted to enter the gates of the heavens. As she ascended into the great light, however, she was kidnapped by Lord Raptor. He took her just before her spirit would have been enveloped by the Almighty, wrapping his sticky hands around her legs and pulling her out of her peaceful slumber.

He delivered Brianna to a room in the Temple of Purgatory, and she was trapped there now, beyond her will and that of the Almighty. She knew that Lord Raptor treated her differently than the other souls in the dungeons below because she was not a nor-mal candidate for Purgatory. Lord Raptor was filled with evil, and he loathed her purity and innocence. He was there at her side, as he is when anyone dies, and stole her soul by surprise.

Brianna knew how evil Lord Raptor was, but she still could not hate him. Brianna was pure in her soul and hate was never a part of her being. Fear was in her heart, but never hate. That was why he chose to snatch her away from the entrance to heaven: because he knew that she would not hate him the way he was despised by every other soul he held captive—from the Almighty God. Somewhere in his consciousness, he missed his beginnings, and his *once upon a time*, goodness.

Brianna was scared, but she was strong. Every day for the last year she had stared out of her barred windows to the Forest of Beauty, hoping that she would someday be set free.

The study was dark and gloomy, as was every other apartment in the Temple of Purgatory. Brianna swallowed in fear as she stood silently at the doorway. Lord Raptor lounged in the polished redwood armchair, snoring from the potent alcohol still clutched in his hands. His long, yellowish-green claws were entwined together, strangling the neck of the brandy decanter, and his head was flung back, uncomfortably leaning on the headrest of his chair. His tongue lolled out the side of his mouth.

Brianna could see the old brass keys to the dungeon hanging askew from the fold in his cloak. She tiptoed carefully to his side. Chills of terror enveloped her as she considered just what she was about to attempt. She glanced again at Lord Raptor's horrible face and saw that his eyes were closed to slits, just showing the pale neon shine of the pupil behind the lid. She knew for certain that he was still asleep—and incredibly drunk.

She remembered something her mother used to say to her father when they were joking and she had just caught him in the act of setting up a trick to tease her.

"Caught you sleeping," her mother would say as she playfully punched her father in the shoulder.

With that wonderful memory, Brianna sucked up all her fear and stretched out her hand. In one motion, she slid the keys from her captor's robe and let them fall into her palm. Lord Raptor stirred briefly, his head bobbing toward the other side of the room on his headrest, snuffling as he moved. She froze for a brief moment and then tiptoed out of the study.

Brianna crept through the kitchen and around to the front hall, which was hardly ever visited. She reached the front door, placed the key in the lock, and opened the door to Micah and another man, both eagerly awaiting her arrival. Beyond them, Brianna could smell the Forest of Beauty for the first time. She filled her lungs with the freshness of the outside world.

Someday, I will go there, thought little Miss Brie.

PURGATORY

They crept silently through the castle, Brianna leading the way. With light, quick steps, she led them down through the dark corridors, deeper and deeper until the very air they inhaled was as dank as the old stone walls. They entered a large room lit with small torches set between holding cells with thick metal bars.

"This is the fourth chamber, Sir Micah. This is where Lord Raptor holds the youngest souls of the lost. You will find Chad, son of Samuel, in the furthest cell to the right. I must wait here, for I cannot go past the threshold of Purgatory," Brianna explained with a curtsey.

"Tell me, Miss Brie, why can't you go further?" Micah asked.

Samuel stood silently behind him, too scared to even think of opening his mouth to ask anything.

"I cannot pass this threshold simply because I am not a spirit of purgatory: I am Lord Raptor's personal slave. He took me before the light could. This is a very powerful place, Sir Micah. It is also monitored by angels. It is they who will not let me pass. It is they who believe that...that someday..." Miss Brie began to cry.

"Someday what, little one?" Micah asked, bending to comfort Brianna.

She crouched, hiding her face, and Micah squatted to put his strong arm about her little shoulders. She felt cold to the touch, and her body shivered. He looked up at Samuel, who was also silently weeping, seemingly unable to comprehend any of this insanity.

Micah did not badger Miss Brie into giving an answer. He thought he knew what she had been trying to say. She would be in for a surprise soon enough, but it would have to wait. They had no time to waste.

"I must thank you," he whispered in her ear. "Let's go, Samuel. Chad is waiting!"

Micah led the way now, Samuel following in his footsteps like a shadow.

"Bear up, man," Micah said. "We are going to free your son—and a part of you as well, I bet."

Samuel straightened his shoulders and sniffed back the remainder of his tears. He had the heart of a soldier, Micah thought.

As they strode over the ancient stones of the Temple floor, they kept their minds tightly focused, shutting out the secrets and regrets that bloomed as profusely as weeds inside every cell they passed. Screams and moans peaked and whispered along the hallway, sending chills up their spines.

Now, at the threshold of Purgatory, they could see images of ghosts in different places and landscapes. Beyond each set of bars, a different scene met their eyes. Micah peered into a nearby cell and saw a woman on a hill above a house in a meadow. She sang a lovely melody that drew Micah helplessly closer. Her face was beautiful. Yet the cold blue of her eyes in her pale face froze Micah to the bone. He managed to free himself of her gaze and kept walking.

Samuel peeked to his left and saw a man looking hopelessly out the window of a dark room, a silky curtain whisking around his face. Beyond the window lay an ocean so dark blue it looked black. The tide flooded the sand before it over and over, making a natural music that began to weigh down Samuel's eyelids. He drew in a breath of damp air and kept moving.

Time and reality seemed to have disappeared when Micah and Samuel reached the threshold of Purgatory. Samuel still followed Micah, although for a moment he forgot exactly what they were doing or where they were. A familiar sight inside a cell they were passing brought everything back. Samuel looked between the bars and saw the inside of his own home: the kitchen, the TV, the dining room table—and Chad, down on his knees scrubbing a stain on the carpet with a bucket of soapy water and a rag.

What a good son, he thought. Samuel moved to embrace Chad in a hug and tell him that he loved him. Instead, he met the unyielding metal of the bars. He held his hand to his head and stared at the scene before him, unconsciously holding his breath. At that moment, he felt the greatest pull of love that he had ever experienced. Samuel could hardly believe the feeling that flooded over him as he silently watched the ghost of his boy working away at his secret task, cleaning his old home while his father was gone, thinking that no one watched.

Samuel tilted his head from side to side, thoughts racing. He thought for a greedy moment that he could stand there and watch his son for eternity, but he hated to see Chad behind bars, trapped in this place that was supposed to purify the souls of the lost. He wondered why his son was being held there, and if he had anything to do with it.

Sir Micah, the Purifier, came to Samuel's side and unlocked the door of the cell with the ancient keys.

"Go to him. It's OK, Samuel. This is what we're here to do. Now, when you approach your son, he will be able to hear you. Make your peace. Say whatever it is you wish to tell him. I may be the Purifier, but I can only open the doors. It is those who transport the love between them that create the purification. It is your time to shine. Now go to him, Samuel…set him free."

Samuel entered the opening in the bars and suddenly felt warmer, not from the torches on the walls, but from that familiar comfort that one can only experience at home. The glow he felt was not from the temperature of the room, but from the memory of having his son safe and content at home with him. This feeling had become a sad memory in his day-to-day life. It had been gone in a moment, like a breath already taken and never to be breathed again. The presence of his family seemed like a day in the sun, a day now gone forever and never to be lived again. At that moment, Samuel knew he had been given back that breath and that day from his past. He collapsed to his knees in front of his son.

"Chad! My boy, can you hear me?"

Chad jerked backward from the spot he was cleaning on the carpet, startled by his father's voice.

"Oh! Da…Da…Dad? What? I was just…"

"Oh my boy! You *can* hear me!" Samuel cried as he circled his arms around his son and pulled him to his chest.

Chad did not ask his father how he was able to do that, he simply began to weep.

"Shh. Shh, my boy. It's all right. Oh my Chad. My son. I should have been a better father to you. I am so sorry, Chad. I am so sorry," murmured Samuel as he clutched the body of his son for the last time.

"Dad, I never should have run away. I should have stayed and helped you with things. I wish I'd been a better son!" Chad cried, his voice taking on the deeper tones of the young man he had started to become in the world of the living. His tears flowed, and he buried his head with its long hair against his father's shoulder.

They held each other close, murmuring words between father and son, words that could never be recorded in any book, alone with each other and in the privacy of their secret prayers that day. The seconds turned into minutes, and light came from nowhere, seeming to fill all the angles of the sky. Samuel did not question or fear the brightness. He just held Chad as his form began to fade from his arms. There were no more words and no more cries. He watched his now sleeping son ascend into the heavens.

"You've done it!" said Micah from behind him.

Samuel turned to face Micah, happy tears dripping down his rugged cheeks.

"I must go now. You must stay here," Micah said.

The dungeon doors were slowly fading away.

"Thank you, Michael Joseph," Samuel said.

"I'll be at work on Monday if you need to find me," Micah said.

He winked at Samuel and disappeared from the room, back down the corridor of the dungeon cells.

Micah returned to the bottom of the stairs, passing the souls who once again reached out to him with their haunted gaze.

When he reached Miss Brie, she was shaking.

"What is it, dear?" he asked, crouching down to meet her eyes.

"Oh, Sir Micah, he is waking. Lord Raptor will wake and surely find us," she whimpered.

They hurried upstairs, through the halls and to the entrance of the castle. All was eerily quiet throughout the Temple. He slid the door open, grasped her hand, and hurried through, pulling her after him.

Just steps outside the door, Micah felt Brianna's hand slip from his. He looked behind him to see her pale arm disappear through the crack in the door just as a long green arm gripping a sword came slashing down with tremendous force, slicing Micah's forearm.

"Ah!" screamed Miss Brie as Lord Raptor yanked her back into the darkness of the Temple. The heavy doors slammed shut as Micah, bending over in pain, fell into the ferns of the forest. He squeezed his wounded left arm against his stomach, hot blood from the deep gash soaking his brown garment.

"No! Brianna..." screamed Micah.

He struggled back up the few steps to the edge of the door frame, writhing in anguish. Above him he could hear the cackle of the crows in the forest, perched and fluttering on the entrance to the Temple. Micah was helpless. He did not care about the deep laceration that burned in his arm. He didn't even feel it anymore— he was too aware of his failure to save Miss Brie. He looked up to the sky and the never-ending branches high above, now shadowed by the ugly black crows. He closed his eyes in exhaustion.

When he opened them, the white wolves were licking his face, and Zelius stood over him, staring down with a concerned frown. Micah closed his eyes again.

When he next opened them, he was in his apartment, first drowning, then coughing, and finally swallowing water from the cup that Zelius had tilted down his throat.

"Did you think I would miss my appointment?" Zelius asked, chuckling in his bigger than life manner. Everything about Zelius was big, his size, his booming voice, his movements, and his commanding presence.

AWAKENING

Sleep came, an unearthly sleep that took Micah far beyond the boundaries of awareness. When he and Samuel awoke from their journey, Zelius gave them both his hospitality within the confines of Micah's apartment. Samuel, in particular, was exhausted. He had traveled to an area between his mind and soul that he didn't even know existed. Not only had Micah taken him to the spiritual realm without any of the proper precautions, but he also left Samuel on his own after he purified Chad's soul, leaving him in a type of black hole. He moved like a zombie, and Zelius insisted that he remain under his care until he felt that he was ready to drive home and transition back into the realm of the living.

Micah, Zelius realized anew, was an individual of unbelievable power. Zelius thought that he knew practically everything there was to know about the powers of the human psyche, and he was proven wrong once again. Zelius could not figure out how Sir Micah had elevated Samuel's mind to the level of his own, taking him on a quest through the wilderness of creation. What an amazing creature. Zelius had never seen him do anything like that before, and he thought that perhaps Micah's powers had evolved beneficially throughout the millenniums.

Yes, Micah was extraordinary, although Zelius couldn't help but feel a slight tinge of irritation. What he had done was very dangerous, or at least Zelius thought so. When he arrived at Micah's godforsaken apartment, he found Micah and his believer, Samuel, engaged in a séance deeper than he had ever seen. In a way, it was a ludicrous sight. They were both floating a few inches above the floor, a wispy haze of incense permeating the room and a spilled bottle of tequila draining on the table. His first thought was that the two had taken drinking to a new level, alien to mankind, but he quickly realized that no normal human could levitate—not with the help of any substance. He positioned them safely for their return and awakened them from their trip.

Samuel eventually moved through the hall, down the stairs, and into his patrol car to drive home in confusion.

Micah succumbed to deep sleep for two days. He awoke at intervals to drink water and eat small portions of food that his nurturing Guardian Angel readied for him. Being in the spiritual realm of the Forest of Beauty had temporarily enhanced Micah's physical and mental agility, but on returning to the realm of the living, he was drained of all his strength. Now fully aware of the powers that he held, he was very excited. He would awaken at times and try to rise to his feet, but Zelius patiently insisted that he continue his slumber until he was ready to begin again.

It was noon on the following Monday when someone knocked loudly on the apartment door. Micah awoke slowly, too late to answer the door himself. Micah sighed, leaving the next instant in God's hands as he saw little Sandy staring bug-eyed at the enormous Zelius. She looked impossibly beautiful.

"Uh, hello. I'm here to see Michael."

She backed up a step, shifting her eyes to neighboring apartment doors, obviously wondering if she had knocked on the right one.

"Hello, my dear. You must be Sandy," Zelius bellowed. "I am Zelius, Micah's Guardian Angel. He will not be coming to work today, if that is what you were going to ask him. You may talk to him if you like. Please come in."

Micah leaned back on his arms, a frown on his brow. He felt like a small, pouting boy next to Zelius. He didn't appreciate this one bit.

"Michael, what's going on with you? Are you OK?" Sandy asked as she moved around the giant.

She knelt down beside Micah on the couch. He couldn't help himself as he looked into her deep green eyes. He cupped her chin gently with his left hand and kissed her, wondering if he imagined that she lingered in the kiss.

"I'm fine, Sandy, except I'm afraid I won't be at work for the next two weeks. I'm—involved—in something important. Uh, do you remember what I told you about being clairvoyant? Well, it's a little more than that…"

Before he could continue, Sandy placed her fingers against his lips and smiled. She glanced up to see Zelius standing tall and quiet, his head only a few inches short of the apartment ceiling.

"You don't need to explain to me, Michael," she said. "I believe you. But when will I see you again?"

"He will see you again in two weeks. You will have a date," Zelius boomed. "I will see to it. Oh, what a delightful sight it is to see two young people blossom like flowers in a new love! But not until then."

Micah pitied himself in that moment, even though he felt a funny kind of warmth for his Guardian Angel. He reached into his coat pocket for the keys to Movie Buff and handed them to Sandy.

"Take care of the shop for now," he said. "Gosh…I…"

Sandy once again shushed him with her fingers on his lips. "I feel it too, Boss," she said smiling and blushing.

"Don't call me that!" Micah said.

Sandy leaned over, kissed him one more time on the cheek, and then moved to the door. "It was nice to meet you, Celio."

Micah kept his eyes locked on Sandy's as she stepped into the hallway and Zelius closed the door.

Balancing like a dreidel, Zelius whirled around on his heels. "I come from heaven, Sir Micah, but I can assure you this is going to be 'hell week' for you," he said with a confident smile.

Micah once again felt like a boy of five, intimidated at starting his first day of kindergarten. He let himself fall back on the couch cushions.

When Zelius told Micah that he was going to put him through hell week, he was not exaggerating. No new football player or military recruit had ever trained as hard, or been driven as mercilessly, as Micah was for two weeks. Zelius drove Micah to his physical limits. First, Zelius forced him to stop drinking entirely, which brought on a mild case of the DTs—delirium tremens, or alcohol detox withdrawals. This lasted two full days and a portion of the third.

Zelius woke Micah at four o'clock every morning with a bowl of hot refried beans and eggs for breakfast. After eating, Micah followed Zelius out of the apartment, down the stairs, and through miles of alleyways, streets, and sidewalks at a fast-paced jog, interfaced with fast sprints.

For the first four days, Micah had to stop at intervals to brace himself against a wall. There were times when Zelius drove him to fits of vomiting.

Occasionally, morning pedestrians observed them running and looked twice at Zelius's towering form. He always led them to the now familiar park behind the Church of the People, where Micah and he had their first new-age encounter. There, Micah had to complete fifteen grueling workout sets: pull-ups on the bars, and three kinds of push-ups on the grassy ground. Zelius roared at him and laughed—an annoyingly loud guffaw—whenever Micah collapsed in the dirt from overexertion.

Although he was firm, Zelius was also encouraging, and Micah gradually began to notice that the intense workouts were becoming easier. His strength and agility increased at an unbelievable rate.

After the sixth day, he could feel new power in his body as it became more synchronized with his mind. Micah was now able to fly through the calisthenics with ease.

On the tenth day, Micah was finishing a mixed set of sit-ups and push-ups when he heard Zelius say, "Look here!" in an alarmed tone.

Micah hopped to his feet to be startled by a hard wooden object flying toward his forehead. Almost instinctively, he caught the object in his hand. He did not have time to study the practice weapon because Zelius was rushing toward him, swinging a stick of his own. At the speed of lightning, Micah broke the slashing trajectory of Zelius's weapon with an upward thrust of his own, creating an echoing crack.

Micah was amazed at his sudden instinctive ability to sword fight. They whacked and cracked their swords, thrusting forward and backward, Micah pivoting his feet with the gracefulness of a ballet dancer. The excitement he felt at his renewed athleticism was nearly unbearable.

"Do you see, now? Do you remember now, Micah? Look at you now, man! You swordfight like Sir Lancelot!" yelled Zelius in delight.

And he did remember. It felt as though he could fight with his eyes closed. The visual memory of his powerful past lives was vague, although his energy had a memory of its own and would be impossible to dismiss. He knew himself better in that moment than ever before in his present life. He was an extraordinary person, a spiritual warrior of good versus evil. He possessed those powers and always had. He was the Purifier.

The days turned into weeks, and finally Zelius gave Micah the OK to rest. Micah's body was tired and his muscles sore, although he felt great and took enjoyment in his enhanced physical appearance. His arms, which had always been strong, were now roped with healthy veins, and his legs seemed to glide more swiftly as he walked.

Zelius also allowed Micah to enjoy a single glass of wine. "You may have one glass, and that is it! If you must drink, then you will learn to do so in a sociable manner," Zelius told him in a calm but concerned voice.

Micah felt guilty as he sipped from his glass. It was not comforting to drink in Zelius's presence, because all the angel did now was watch him with his hazel eyes. During the past day or so, Zelius had seemed distant, deep in thought and not cheerful as he had been at the beginning.

Both men were chilling out in the apartment, each assuming their usual position—Micah reclining on the couch, Zelius barely fitting into a chair across from him.

Micah decided to bring the estranged communication between them to a head. "What's troubling you, Zelius?"

Zelius stared out the window, his thick golden locks draped around his shoulders and covering his broad neck. He turned to gaze at Micah, smiling suddenly.

"I just hope you are ready."

Micah closed his eyes. A moment later, when he opened them, Zelius had once again disappeared.

MICAH'S FATHER

A monsoon thunderstorm ripped the sky with lightning, punctuated by the ominous rumble of thunder. Soon the sky filled with sheeting rain. The thirsty cut grass brushed, healthy and firm, beneath the soles of Micah's shoes as he walked through it. By the time he had walked a few feet from his car, he was drenched. Unconcerned, he turned his head toward the sky, inviting the water to soak his hair and face, letting the rain wash away his tears.

Kneeling, his knees molded shallow grooves in the wet ground before the rectangular gray stone marking his father's resting place. The rain continued to beat down in the Cemetery of Hope, where his father was buried a year ago. Micah raised his head from time to time. The downpour flooding his eyes blinded him, but he knew he was alone in the cemetery. It was peaceful, and he heard only the rain dripping from the leaves. The trees scattered throughout the cemetery grounds seemed to silently watch him through their shroud of mist.

On the lonely days that Micah came to visit his father's grave, the things he wanted to say felt truly deep. But when he tried to speak, the words on his mind slipped out in false starts and fragmented sentences and they ended up not sounding very deep at all.

Guess what, Dad? Micah always waited a moment for the questions he asked his father to be answered in his mind.

No bottle with me today!

He waited, listening as he kneeled, hands in his lap. He began counting the seconds between the lightning flash and the distant rumble of thunder. His sodden clothing would have to go to the laundry later.

You know, Dad, you gave me plenty of things to cherish in my life, and as much as I don't want to give this back to you, I have to.

He reached into his pocket and brought out the special antique flask that his father had given him. He placed it gently on the grass, resting it against the bottom of the gravestone. He knew that his father would have more than understood. As he looked at the old silver flask now resting in its new home, he knew his father was not in Purgatory. When Micah closed his eyes to listen to the spatter of rain again, he could see his father smile.

MICAH AND SANDY

The rain subsided to a shallow popping sound on the pavement outside Micah's car windows. He hummed softly as he drove through the streets toward Sandy's house. His muscles were tight and his physical appearance clean cut. It was an exciting night. It had been two long weeks since he and Sandy last saw each other, and tonight they would go on their first date.

His hair was trimmed, his mind was clear, and he was falling in love. He drove on the highway between the long cornfields to Sandy's house with a smile on his face. He was so much happier now that he had begun to realize his true self.

Pulling up outside of Sandy's old house, he could see her shadow passing frequently back and forth before the lighted windows. The little house looked livelier tonight than it had the first time he visited, the porch light casting a welcoming pool of light. Micah thought that Sandy would be excited to see him, too. He honked the horn and watched as her lovely shadow stopped in place, alert as a deer in headlights. She came to the living room window, moving the curtain aside to peer out at him.

He was going to jump out and run up to her porch to greet her, but she opened the door and came hurrying toward the passenger side of his car. He reached across to open the door for her and she climbed inside, her auburn hair shining and green eyes sparkling as they looked into his with delight.

"Hi!" she said.

Micah let his eyes scan her body confidently before saying, "Well hello there pretty lady." He paused to light a cigarette before asking, "Are you sure we're OK to go out for a while? Where's Robby? How is he?"

"Thank you for asking, Micah," Sandy said, leaning over to kiss his cheek. "He's doing really well today. He's…"

She was abruptly interrupted as Robby called and waved from the porch.

"Hey, Micah, hey!" he yelled, nearly jumping up and down as he waited to be acknowledged. He looked pale but happy. "Hey, my sis is cool to go out tonight. Take her. Go, go! She's more boring than Grandma right now."

"Hey!" Sandy yelled back at him.

"All right, Rob. I'm counting on you to take care of yourself tonight, bud. I'm taking your sister out," Micah yelled out the car window so Robby could see his face.

"OK, bye," Robby said and entered the house, closing the door behind him.

"He's a good kid. I really like him," Micah said.

He rolled Sandy's window down before he exhaled more smoke. She smelled like wildflowers, and now he felt as though he should never have lit a cigarette.

"You smell so good," he said.

"On the contrary, I smell like cigs now, wise guy."

Micah's jaw dropped and then curved into another smile as she reached for the pack of Marlboro Reds and lit her own smoke with the lighter in her purse.

"I guess I better be on my best behavior tonight," he said, blowing a fresh smoggy cloud out the window as he drove away from the house.

"You better," she replied, placing her soft hand over the top of Micah's.

Sandy was dressed up in a casual yet very flattering outfit. The black skirt was fashionably short, and her outstanding legs were sexy in an athletic way, smooth and tan. The green-painted toenails of her slim feet peeked through the leather net of her sandal tops. She wore a soft, ruffled green sleeveless top that matched her eyes. Her hair was tied in a bun on the back of her head, behind a perfect wave of bangs fringing her forehead. She looked confident, put together, and ridiculously sexy.

"You look beautiful, Sandy. Your hair..."

"Thank you," she whispered in his right ear.

Before Micah knew it, he was trying to watch the road while making out with Sandy.

He took her to Red Wings, a familiar and friendly restaurant he knew she would enjoy. It was appropriate for the night as it served gourmet buffalo chicken wings, great pizza, and alcohol—which he vowed to drink only in extreme moderation. The ambience at Red Wings was relaxed, filled with the sound of dishes being placed on different surfaces, the laughter of happy customers, and the excellent aromas of bubbling tomato sauces.

Micah and Sandy walked in hand in hand, and the waiter seated them in a perfect corner booth looking over the street outside. The calm silences between their conversations were comfortable, the ice broken by the friendly talking voices taking place all around them.

Sandy decided that she wanted wine with dinner, and Micah ordered them two glasses of a fine deep-red Zinfandel, which he thought she would enjoy. From the way Sandy held her wine glass, he could tell that she was not an experienced drinker—which was good, because it would not have been encouraging for him to find out that Sandy drank like her grandmother.

"You know, Sandy, I would have ordered a bottle for us to share, but I'm trying to cut down a little," Micah said.

"I'm glad you didn't. This stuff is strong, and I'm feeling buzzed already. I just might think you were trying to get in my pants if you ordered a whole bottle!" she said as she took a sip from the glass.

Micah cleared his throat, and she looked up, smiled at him, and then hiccupped. She was a lightweight, and dangerously seductive. *Oh boy!*

The two glasses Micah had ordered turned into another two by the end of dinner. Sandy was light- hearted and funny. As the night continued, he became aware of how easy it was to talk to Sandy. She listened and responded more maturely than he expected. In fact, she really knew a lot about so many things. She loved books, and read biographies and historical novels, as well as mysteries and romance. As she talked, strands of her hair fell freely over her pretty eyes, and she indulged in her meal with pleasure, buffalo sauce collecting in little bits at the corners of her mouth. She was down to earth and—even being as pretty as she was—she didn't seem to give a flying fuck if she had a little sauce on her chin.

Micah noticed that he was smiling goggle-eyed at her while she ate hungrily.

"What?" Sandy asked as she looked up from her nearly clean plate.

She smiled suddenly, as if she had caught Micah's thoughts. She reached into her purse, beside her on the booth seat, and retrieved a small makeup mirror. She flicked the little mirror open and started laughing, a remarkable soft sound.

"Oh my God, Micah. Why didn't you tell me?" she said, dabbing her mouth with her napkin.

"Because you look just as pretty, if not prettier, with sauce on your face."

He finished off his second glass of wine, put it down, and gazed at her hungrily. She responded with a playful and somehow very sexy frown of disapproval.

Back at Sandy's front door, she wrapped her legs around him as he picked her up and pinned her against the porch wall. They made out until Micah put her back on her feet and stepped back to look at her. Suddenly, the light nearest the windows where they stood came on, cutting short their moment of tipsy passion.

"Sandy, honey, is that you out there?"

The door opened, and her grandmother came out onto the porch. Sandy sighed and posed herself appropriately.

"Yes, Gram," she said. "I want you to meet my bo--- boss, Micah. Micah, this is my Grandmother."

"Hello," Micah said, sticking out his hand.

Sandy's Grandmother looked him up and down for a brief moment and then smiled approvingly as she shook his hand. Her skin was soft and wrinkled.

"Well, dear, he sure is handsome," she said.

"Gram!"

"You're quite easy to look at yourself, Miss Grandma" Micah said.

Sandy's grandma didn't care what she had interrupted on the front porch. She was still a grandmother.

They all went inside for coffee, Sandy obviously wishing for a bit more time alone. For Micah, however, it was all working out perfectly. He thought of himself as gallant, and he wanted to keep it that way.

"Are you sure you have to leave tonight?" Sandy asked in her sexiest voice as she followed Micah out to the porch.

"It will be best that way. I need to get going. Plus, after all the ruckus we made, I can't believe Robby's still sleeping. I'm afraid that if I stayed the night, we'd wake him up for sure—you know what I'm saying?" Micah asked with a grin.

"Yeah, I guess so."

"He needs to get his sleep tonight," he said and pulled Sandy in close. Sandy's arms lingered around his body as he turned to walk down the porch steps to his Volvo. He smiled.

"Micah," Sandy said as he was halfway down the path.

"Hey," he replied.

"That was a killer date."

"I'm still your boss, you know," Micah said.

He winked and got in his car, Sandy stood on the porch watching until he was out of sight. He drove back toward his apartment with excitement coursing through his veins. The moon was covered by clouds, making the sky black as pitch. He rolled up his window as it began to rain again.

He didn't need a smoke, but he lit one anyway.

THE DEMON AND ROBBY

Grandma had, for the first time in ages, gone to sleep in her little bedroom at the end of the hallway next to Robby's room. Sandy sat at the kitchen table, pondering the events of the night and thinking about the wonderful way Micah made her feel. She knew that he was attracted to her. There was no doubt about that.

The aftereffects of the wine and his sudden departure made her mind spin and her loins warm with sexual thoughts. She was just about to drift into a doze in the kitchen chair when she heard a knock at the door. Her body felt tired, but a mildly exciting amusement pushed her up from the chair. She hoped to find Micah waiting for her on the porch.

She ran her fingers through her hair a couple of times, not sure what she was accomplishing. Robby and her grandmother were asleep, so she pulled off her top to answer the door in her bra, as if just getting ready for bed. She whipped the door open. It wasn't Micah.

"Oh my God! Excuse me," she gasped as she pushed the door lock and grabbed her blouse, hastily pulling it on before opening the door again.

106

"Hello?" she said.

The man standing there was tall and skinny, dressed in a medical doctor's white coat. A stethoscope hung around his neck. The man's skin was pale, with an odd blue tinge. She imagined it was probably just from the porch light, but Sandy was alarmed by the unusual yellowish color of the man's eyes.

"Hello, Miss. You must be Sandy. Robby has told me all about you. I am his new doctor, Dr. Tore." The man smiled and held out his hand.

Sandy reluctantly shook it. His skin felt cold and clammy, and his hand lay limp in her own. She didn't like him.

"What's the problem, Doctor? Robby's asleep, and..."

"I'm glad to hear that he is sleeping, Miss, though I am afraid I have some bad news, and it calls for urgent attention. I know it is late, but the tests we ran the other day confirm that your little brother is suffering from a severe case of viral pneumonia. His lungs are slowly filling with a certain fluid that is dangerous. It is asymptomatic at first but can escalate very rapidly to become life-threatening. I rushed here right away. I feel I must see the boy at once," Dr. Tore said.

Despite the seriousness of the situation, a grin flitted across his thin lips. It was almost as though he were trying to sell her something.

I must be tripping, thought Sandy. She wasn't expecting such terrible news, but the doctor must be sincere because it was so late. She shook her uneasy feelings aside.

"Please come inside and follow me to Robby's room."

She expected the doctor to thank her, but he was silent as he followed her quietly down the hallway. When they entered Robby's room, she was startled to hear him wheezing. She switched on the light, noting that the doctor's head almost reached the top of the door frame.

"Sissy," murmured Robby, the nickname he had given her when he was still a baby.

"Robby, bubba, what happened? You're wheezing again, aren't you?" Sandy asked as she knelt down to his chest.

Robby backed up onto his pillow, exclaiming in terror, "Who's that guy?"

Sandy thought he must be delirious again. It sometimes happened when his pneumonia flared up. Before she could speak, she felt a hand brace her shoulder and looked up.

"May I?" asked Dr. Tore.

Sandy got up and moved out of the way, letting the doctor take her place.

"You remember me, Robby. I'm Dr. Tore," he said as he took the stethoscope from around his neck.

"No, I don't remember you. Sissy!"

Robby tried to look over the man's shoulder, but the doctor applied enough pressure with the stethoscope on Robby's chest to keep him from moving.

"It's OK, Rob. He's here to help—right, Dr. Tore?" said an uncertain Sandy, trying to reassure Robby.

"Heh, heh, yes, yes. Oh, indeed. I am here to help," the doctor said, his voice beginning to change.

Before Sandy's horrified gaze, his suit turned into a long back cloak that trailed his body all the way to where Sandy stood. Robby began to scream as the man transformed into a demon before his eyes. Dr. Tore's fingers stretched long and pointy under bumpy green skin.

"Hush, hush now, boy. It will only be for eternity. Ha-ha!" the demon said as he placed his long ugly claws over Robby's forehead.

The boy became silent at once. The demon stood, raising his arms as if to call all the forces of evil to his aid.

Sandy screamed as Robby froze, and Lord Raptor spun around to grin at her. His horrible yellow eyes burned into her soul. The demon towered over her like an apparition from her most terrifying nightmare. She stared in horror as he grinned, his teeth becoming large incisors, sharply stretching his evil smile from ear to ear.

A storm had erupted outside. It roared, pushing gusts of rain and wind against the sides of the house and rattling the window-panes with its force. A sudden flash of lightning lit up the room and the bone-chilling sight of the monster before her.

"My name is Lord Raptor, miss, but you may call me Dr. Demon. Ha-ha!" he screeched.

He gripped her around the neck, his claws choking her. His long purple snake of a tongue came unraveling from deep inside his sharp mouth to slip and slide across her face, leaving a foul slime on her cheeks.

The demon threw her against the wall like a rag doll, and she hit her head, collapsing with a helpless cry. Grandma, awakened by the commotion, entered the room swinging a large broomstick at him. He slapped her impatiently to the floor, where she stayed.

"I must be going now, Sandy. Please excuse me. I gave the Purifier a chance to stay dormant, but he chose to use his powers again. He will lose now no matter what; that's how it will go. But if you don't want your brother to die with him, tell Micah that he must hand his soul over to me."

ROBBY'S SOUL

Robby lay in a coma in the hospital. The doctors were unable to figure out what had happened, but Micah knew. Sandy was also in the hospital, with a mild concussion from her head injury. Although the wound was not life-threatening, it needed medical attention. Her real injury was the aftermath of the traumatizing event that her brave little family had experienced because of Micah.

Sandy's grandmother had been beaten to the carpet of her dead daughter's home. While her wounds would eventually heal, her broken heart might not be able to mend. She was now mute in a hospital room next to Sandy's.

Every time Sandy awoke from her drug-induced sleep, she moaned for Robby. The nurses always gave her the same answer. She could barely look Micah in the eyes. She did not want to blame him, but she had not said more than a sentence to him that had any meaning. Her eyes wandered, glassy and bulging. She was incoherent as much from emotional pain and worry as from the side effects of pain-killers.

Micah sat in a chair next to Robby's bed, his right arm touching Robby's to let him know he was there. He felt drained, and his stupid powers seemed absolutely useless at the moment. He looked around to see if any nurses were coming before pulling the half-pint of Patrón from his coat pocket and swallowing down two swigs. He replaced the metal cap and fit the small bottle back into his coat pocket. He closed his eyes and began to dream, his past winding down behind his eyelids.

His father was in his dream, the sky blue and the air clear. The ocean was calm as far as the eye could see. They were no longer on the shore but out in the ocean now. Micah could see where he and his father were headed, and their destination was no longer as far away.

As a boy, he had always listened to his father. His father knew things. There was no questioning him, but Micah never wanted to do so anyway. His answers were always clear. Micah never saw himself in these dreams, so he never knew whether he was a small boy or a grown man. That didn't matter either, because in his father's presence he was always a boy, always his father's son. As Micah watched, he knew that his father was smiling, a smile warm enough to heat the room.

He could not see the boat beneath them, but he did not need to. They were safe above the water, and that was all he needed to understand. His smiling father pointed toward the magnificent island in the near distance. This time it was much clearer. It drew his gaze as if through magnetism. The glow of the sun overhead made the dew sparkle on the green shell of living foliage surrounding the one and only Forest of Beauty.

As Micah made his way home that day, he felt all alone. Lord Raptor took away from him the most precious things in his renewed life. The demon had entered the realm of the living, snatching Robby's soul and taking it with him into the darkness of the Temple of Purgatory. The boy would soon succumb to true death if Micah did not turn his own soul over to the demon.

Micah repeated numerous times that there was nothing the police could do, but Samuel had deployed every unit of his police force throughout the town to search for the violent intruder who had attacked Sandy and her family. He remained a loyal friend and tried to do everything he could possibly think of to help.

The monsoon thunderstorms had been intermittent for several days now, flooding the gutters, washing and cleansing the pavement, and changing the colors of the sky to match the buildings in a dark flush. Micah felt selfish as he drove home through the deserted streets of the small Arizona town. He had let Sandy down. All he ever wanted to do was make things happy for her and Robby.

He knew what he had to do now, but he could not even tell himself his reason for being so selfish. It was his fault that her family was hurt. It was his fault that Robby was in such danger, and that Sandy and her grandmother's lives were in such danger of being ruined. If Robby died, then Micah would die too. But all he wanted to do was drink. He had fucked up again. He might as well get to drinkin'.

"Fuck it!" he said as he slid down the brick wall behind Henry's Liquor, soaking his pants in the water and muck of the alley. He finished the tequila that remained at the bottom of his bottle.

He watched dizzily as a fire department ambulance rushed by, skidding and splashing spiral waves of water from underneath its tires. He let his chin droop on his chest as his troubles swam depressingly through his mind. Becoming nauseated from too much booze was now Micah's goal every time he drank. That way he knew that he could purge himself of his misery and start again, to feel the high and lose the sadness, for a little while anyway.

He began to drift off when a siren sounded annoyingly close by. He looked up to see Samuel behind the wheel of his police car, Zelius squeezed into the front passenger seat. The angel's hair hung in sodden, dark-gold locks, plastered to the front of his chest.

Samuel stopped the car beside him, leaning out to demand, "Can you get in yourself, or do we have to carry your sorry ass and dump it in the back seat?"

"What is it that ails you, man? Tell me!" bellowed Zelius. "Or better yet, *don't* tell me. I do not wish to hear your false reasoning. It is obvious! You are feeling sorry for yourself again."

Micah climbed into the back seat of the car, and it pulled out into the alley. Micah began vomiting.

"Oh, shit!" Samuel exclaimed.

"You see, man? You drink yourself half to death every blasted time," Zelius yelled.

"Blahg! Ugh, fuck!" Micah moaned as his stomach purged again.

"We are going to do what we are destined to do," shouted Zelius. "That bloody Lord Raptor will pay for this!"

Micah's apartment was cold and damp smelling, though once Zelius ducked through the door into the room, the temperature warmed. Samuel and Zelius immediately began setting up the room for a séance. Within moments, the candles were lit and the incense burning. Samuel prayed in the World of the Living while Micah and Zelius readied themselves for their journey to the Temple of Purgatory.

Micah needed to reach a state of trance before he could venture to the realm of spirituality. He smoked a cigarette as he leaned back on his sofa, blowing silent fog into the dim light. A shaking Samuel sat across from him, and Zelius stood in the corner as he usually did, looking serious and unyielding. The presence of Zelius always had a sobering effect on Micah, and he soon became more coherent and felt better. His phone rang. He knew it was probably Sandy, worried and wondering where he was, but none of them answered. Zelius yanked the cord from the wall, and there was no more noise.

Micah inhaled the pungent scent of the incense he had come to know so well. Just as he reached the space between, he felt the large hands of Zelius embrace his shoulders. He felt himself propelled by a force so dramatic that Micah felt its power throb through every limb in his body, full and pure. They soared above the trees like birds, the wind icy cold on his cheeks. He moved at a breakneck speed, and had Zelius not been guiding his soul, he would have collided with the branches of the enormous trees in the Forest of Beauty. They flew over and then under the forest, and Micah whistled as they glided over the white wolves frolicking on the ground below.

Back at the hospital, the nurses rushed back and forth into Robby's room, watching the heart monitor carefully as his heart rate fluctuated.

He cried, scared and alone in a strange place, lying on a pile of moldy hay. He didn't know where he was or why he was being punished. He could not tell what time it was or how long he had been here. He missed his Sissy. That horrible creature had brought him here to this dungeon, where the rats crawled between the bars and the air stank. It was so dark he couldn't see his own hand when he held it out in front of his face. He had difficulty breathing and knew he was having a pneumonia flare-up. He should probably be in the hospital. Robby wondered if maybe he had died, just as Sissy always feared when he got really sick.

"Robby? Hello?" a girl's soft voice called from beyond the cold bars he had felt with his hands earlier.

Not Sissy, Robby thought, but he couldn't really be sure.

"Hello?" he answered.

"It's OK, Robby. I have brought you some milk," she said.

Robby could not see her, but at that moment, he realized he was very thirsty He held out his hand to retrieve the cup she extended through the bars, and their fingers touched. Her hand was soft and cold.

"Thank you," Robby said. "Who are you?"

"I am Brianna," she said. "I'm trapped here, too, but—unlike you—I am dead."

"Where am I?"

"You are in the Temple of Purgatory. You are in a coma, and I am not sure how Lord Raptor is keeping you here, but he is."

"Lord Raptor? The Temple of Purgatory?" asked Robby "But I'm…"

The light from the torches along the hallway flared suddenly, revealing the demon draped in his most luxurious garments.

"You are going to stay with me forever, is what you are!" roared Lord Raptor. "And you too, Miss Bitch!"

He moved down the steps to grab first Brianna and then Robby, holding them both off the ground by the collars of their shirts.

POOL OF LIFE

They landed swiftly on their feet, side by side: Micah the Purifier and Zelius, his Guardian Angel. They felt no fear. Zelius stood as tall and fearless as ever, and if there had been any anxiety present in Micah's consciousness, it had now turned into a brave call unlike anything he had ever known. The Forest of Beauty seemed to welcome them both in its silent knowing way, and Micah stood, once again inhaling the naturally perfumed scent of the world around him.

Zelius and Micah took a minute to adjust to their surroundings. A beautiful sword hung from Zelius's belt, one that Micah had never seen before. Micah looked down to admire his own attire: he was clothed in the brilliant white garment of a nobleman from the Middle Ages. He noticed a long pink scar trailing down his left arm, from his elbow to his wrist, and remembered his last personal encounter with Lord Raptor. This made him wonder what might have happened if he had received a more serious wound.

"This way," Zelius said.

They did not land in the same place that he and Samuel had when they were in the Forest of Beauty. This time Micah found himself in a grove of trees, butterflies hovering in the air around him. Their vibrant, brilliant colors turning the sky into a rainbow.

The butterflies fluttered above the opening of a sort of natural cave formed by bushy plants and trees. The cave had the feeling of a sacred place, and Micah felt a wave of distant memory as he followed Zelius through the growth at its entrance.

"Do you remember where you are now, Micah?" Zelius asked.

"I...I...think so," he said.

Suddenly a white wolf came leaping over him, running ahead under the roof of the cave. He followed it until they came to a clearing with a small, deep pool of clear blue water in the center.

"The Pool of Life," he whispered.

The little pool was surrounded by forest so dense that they had to squeeze themselves between the trees, through spaces of no more than one or two feet.

Micah knew this was the sacred Pool of Life because this was where the memories of his spiritual soul flooded into his mind. Beneath the water, the shimmering pebbles seemed to call his name and wink at him happily. He knelt down to feel the cool water on his fingertips and brought a handful up to touch his lips.

The white wolf busily sniffed him up and down as Micah squatted beside the pool. The wolf looked at the pool and then jumped, leaping forward to splash and swim to the center. Micah laughed as water splashed his face, and then he dove after the wolf. Under the water, he could see every object, every shade of light that was present on the bottom of the pool.

He could glide and breathe in the cool water of the Pool of Life. It was just like breathing air. He was a fish, a dolphin. He was the water, a human, the soil, the forest. He was pure in this place—in the Pool of Life, in the Forest of Beauty. He knew then that the evil forces of the realm of the living had steered him away from what he knew to be certain in his heart. He descended toward a shining object on the pool's bottom, something that seemed nearly blinding in its radiance. He reached down, grabbing it, and spun his body back to the surface. The wolf barked in glee and stared, mesmerized, at Micah as he held his old sword up to the sky.

Zelius stood chuckling on the bank.

THE BATTLE

Micah and Zelius stood at the edge of the clearing that surrounded the Temple of Purgatory. The white wolf sat whimpering and barking between them at the side of the path ahead of them.

"Shh," whispered Zelius, placing his palm on the wolf's head. "This is it, Sir Micah. We must stop him."

"I know," Micah said, nodding his head at Zelius and boldly making his way to the door. Crows still perched on the arch above, gawking at them.

Micah stopped at the door to the Temple, waited a moment, and knocked furiously. He stood still, listening, his pulse pumping loudly in his skull. He looked over at Zelius, now crouched behind a tree with his sword unsheathed and ready. Zelius must not be seen by Lord Raptor: Micah would have to resolve the situation himself. It was Robby's only chance.

Suddenly the door swung violently open, throwing Micah backward to the ground, his legs and arms flailing in the air. Lord

Raptor loomed in the doorway, holding Robby and Brianna in his claws. The children screamed and kicked.

"What do you plan to do now, you helpless man? I will have you all. Ha-ha!" screeched Lord Raptor in a mind-numbing howl.

"No, you won't, you fucking freak," Micah shouted as he jumped to his feet.

"Perfect," Lord Raptor hissed. "Take the babies. I want *you.*"

He let Robby and Brianna fall to the ground, and they both scurried away from the demon.

Lord Raptor reached behind his voluminous cape and drew out the largest serrated blade that Micah had ever seen. The demon held the sword out to his side, lifted his head, and sniffed the air.

"Is it pretty out? It smells like flowers—and I hate flowers," he growled as he shoved himself off the walkway stone, catching air and landing two feet in front of Micah.

Micah unsheathed his own sword. It had been a century or more since his palm had gripped the old handle, but it seemed like only yesterday.

"You dare to tease me?" asked Lord Raptor.

He came at Micah with a powerful thrust and then another. Micah was ready for him. All of his training and angel boot camp started to kick in. Micah slashed back and forth with his mighty sword. The weight of his weapon felt good in his strong hands. He could win this.

The demon swung his weapon in rapid whirls, coming within a finger's width of Micah's face. Micah tried to fend him off by matching his every swing. Metal clanged and sang against metal, and he had to back up one pace at a time. Lord Raptor, however was becoming too much for him. It had been too long since Micah had engaged in a real sword fight, a fight to the death. He swayed from side to side until he could take no more. Tired to the point of collapse, Micah fell on his back. He was going to die in the realm of the living if Lord Raptor killed his soul in the realm of spirituality.

"Zelius! Help me!" he finally cried.

"Who?" an alarmed Lord Raptor yelled as he raised his sword for a downward thrust.

"You know who. Your old friend, of course." Zelius smiled as he appeared from behind the trees, a pack of twenty white wolves in his wake.

Lord Raptor looked scared, an expression Micah had never witnessed on the demon's face. Before he could raise his sword to deliver the final blow, the white wolves of the Forest of Beauty attacked. They tore at the demon's green flesh, spitting chunks out of their mouths as if it tasted foul. Slowly, as though time stood still, the body of the demon disappeared as the wolves hurled his awful limbs in every direction. Finally, the pack leader, who had guided Micah in the forest, dropped the demon's head at Micah's feet for his approval.

The demon could no longer speak another word; the wolves had taken him like piranhas on a cow. Brianna and Robby sat huddled together beneath a tree, staring at the gruesome scene.

Micah knelt down before them. "Robby, we must go. You need to say good-bye to Miss Brie. You will see her again someday.

"But…but she…" Robby's eyes filled with tears.

Brianna smiled and kissed his cheek, and he let her go.

Micah and Robby watched as Brianna ran with the wolves, who were now prancing playfully around her. She did not look back as she moved through the trees, brushing her delicate hands against the fern fronds. She disappeared into the forest, and the last wolf looked back one more time before loping in after her.

Zelius was nowhere to be seen.

Robby coughed and spat when the doctor removed the ventilator from his throat. He opened his eyes to see a hospital room filled with people circling his bed. The early-morning light shone through the window, illuminating a large pot of red-and-yellow flowers. His sister and grandmother were grinning with happiness.

Robby's thinking was foggy for a moment as he tried to remember exactly where he was. Then he recalled the demon and the dungeon. He remembered his ghostly friend, Brianna, and the way she felt against him when they hugged, cold and fragile. He especially remembered the cool jungle forest that Micah and he had escaped through after the white wolves killed the demon, Lord Raptor. The wolves were so vicious when they attacked, but so protective and sweet to good people. Oh, what a dream it was. He almost wished he could go back, but his family was here in the realm of the living.

"Oh Robby. Oh Bubba," cried his sister as she wrapped him in her arms. She was crying harder than he had ever seen her. He saw bruises on his grandmother's old, pretty face.

"Grandma, what happened to your face?" he asked as she pressed her head against his shoulder.

He ran his hand across his sister's head and felt the bandage and swelling.

"Sissy, what happened to your head?"

"Hey, kiddo, it's all over now," Micah said as he lovingly squeezed Robby's arm.

He rose from the chair beside Robby's bed, noting the expressions of awe on the faces of the room's occupants. A smiling nurse held a cup of water to Robby's mouth as another took out one, then two, of his IV tubes.

Robby suddenly felt rested and good. He breathed in deeply, the most filling breaths of air he had ever experienced. The body heat from Sissy and Grandma made him feel too warm, but he didn't say anything—their touch felt so good. He was beginning to realize that he had come very close to death.

The thought frightened him, and safe here in the love of his family, he began to cry. At twelve years old, Robby knew he was too big to cry. He was afraid he sounded dumb, like a little boy. He tightened his jaw and puffed out his cheeks, trying to control the tears, and felt Micah's hand pat the matted hair on the top of his head. He missed his daddy and mommy, and this felt so good.

He wondered if his parents were in that same beautiful, heavenly forest he had seen in his dream. He certainly felt closer to them there.

When Micah brushed Robby's hair with his heavy hand, Robby just let go and wept.

It was a sight for all to appreciate—the young boy, his loving sister and doting grandmother joyfully whispering to him, and the man who had become their protector and part of their circle of love. They were now four of a kind.

A NEW FAMILY

"Sandy, honey, I don't want to," Micah said, assuming his puppy-dog face. If he frowned and pushed his lower lip out at her just enough to make her smile, she just might forget what she had been thinking.

"Oh no you don't, Michael Joseph! You're going right now—if you have any hopes of me dropping Robby off at his friend's house tonight."

Micah and Sandy were more in love than ever. Over the past year, things between them had become serious; their future together was set in stone. They worked together, lived together in Sandy's house, and never grew tired of each other's company. How glorious it was to be in love like that!

Sandy sat cross-legged on the stool behind the cash register at the Movie Buff. Micah watched her toes wiggle in her thong sandals. He moved his eyes up her smooth legs to her high-cut jean shorts. Sandy bounced her naked foot in its sandal and adjusted her bra strap under her tight summer T-shirt. She didn't need to look at Micah to know how she was affecting him. She flicked a lock of her hair that had meandered over her breasts back over her shoulder and continued to ignore Micah. There was no winning.

"Fuck...OK, love. You sure you're good?" Micah asked.

"Yes, I'm sure. Now, get going, baby. It starts at eleven o'clock," Sandy said.

"All right. Adios, amigo," Micah said.

He was quoting—quite poorly—a line from their favorite movie, *Point Break*. They both loved the scene where Patrick Swayze as Bodhi dove backward from the stunt plane to escape from Keanu Reeves. Before Micah left, he tightened himself in a lover's knot over Sandy's shoulders and pressed his lips to her neck. She was warm and smelled fucking amazing. He lingered until she turned to kiss him.

Micah drove down the streets of the small Arizona town. He ran his tongue over his lips to savor Sandy's sweet lip gloss and then lit a smoke and turned on the shitty air conditioning in his Volvo. It was August, and the heat was sweltering. He wore a pair of board shorts and a new pair of Vans tennis shoes with white ankle socks. He turned on one of his favorite rock albums by the Misfits as he drove in the direction of the Church of the People.

He didn't know why he felt so nervous, but he did. He sat for a moment, finishing his cigarette and studying the people gathered in the park behind the church. He had practiced sword fighting with Zelius in that park, but these people couldn't know that—because they didn't know him. For some reason, that knowledge was comforting.

He would see Sandy in a few hours, and Robby and Grandma would be home as well. His new family. The butt of the cigarette began burning his fingertips, and he flicked it into the Volvo's ashtray.

"Fuck it," he said under his breath as he got out of the car.

He thought about how proud his father would be to see him now. Of course, Micah knew now, he *could* see his son—in a way.

He strolled over to the group and sat down in the circle a minute late—or was it at the perfect time?

They gathered around him, and he said, "My name is Micah, and I'm an alcoholic. I need to be purified."

They laughed.

JEREMY

J eremy lay, eyes open, on his hospital bed.
  "It won't be long," he heard a nurse say.
  Jeremy could not close his eyes or move his mouth. The stroke had paralyzed his body, but his mind was free. He remembered his wife, his son, his life—and although things were rough, he didn't want to go. He didn't want it all to be over. He feared what was next. Suddenly, he felt the goose bumps on his arms smooth out as warmth crept over him. His heartbeat slowed as a man began to speak to him. Suddenly he felt safe, and he knew that everything would be OK. The man had said so.
  "The ducks on the pond will swim like they always have. The trees will sway in the wind. It is not over, Jeremy. You will go on, as does everything else. Prepare yourself for the love and the laughter that is yet to come."

THE GUARDIAN ANGEL

Zelius strode through the desolate halls of the abandoned
Temple of Purgatory. The echoes of his movements were the
only sounds to be heard. He eventually made his way to the dungeons of the lost souls. Zelius was not and never had been a fan of
Purgatory; maybe it was because he believed in freedom from all
negativity, or because he was too kind or too soft-hearted. Perhaps
that was one of the reasons he had not yet been permitted to ascend to the next golden step beyond the Forest of Beauty.

Nevertheless, this was his chance to intervene as he told Micah
he would do. He would engage in the battle of good and evil—and
yes, that particular subject was a constant project for a working
Guardian Angel. What Zelius had ultimately hoped to accomplish
was now at his fingertips.

It was his pleasure as an angel to break the lock off the barred
door of every dark and lonely cell in the Temple. Zelius was pretty
sure that he was bending some of the Almighty God's rules by taking this task upon himself, but he did not like locked doors and
bars, and his reason told him that he should take action.

He could not take over the Temple of Purgatory for his own, nor could he purify souls—nor did he wish to spend a single moment longer than he had to in this creepy place. Who would watch over these lost spirits and document their well-being? It could not be him. One day Sir Micah the Purifier might return and manage the forgotten Temple, but that would not happen until he was finished with his mission in the realm of the living.

So Zelius would do what angels do best: to help and to accomplish miracles. There were probably things that were not yet straightened out with each of the lost spirits, but at least they would now have the option to leave the chambers created by the evil demon. As Zelius passed by, he glanced at the beings who watched him set them free—a lonesome lover here, a sad old woman there. No matter the depressing situations of the apparitions that Zelius saw, it made him happy when at last every dungeon door stood wide open.

Little by little, the ghosts seemed to understand what had happened.

He left the entry doors open, along with every window of the Temple. He stood back to admire his work and thought about inviting Miss Brie to watch but knew she would have chosen not to.

Over time, the greenery would creep its way over the steps and pad the floors of the Temple with moss. The curious vines would explore the interior rooms and spread over the walls until the Temple of Purgatory became just another part of the Forest of Beauty—as Zelius thought it ultimately should be.

The Beginning

AUTHOR'S NOTE

 Not every story has a happy ending, but the stories that end with a sour taste are—for me at least—not entirely over. Words can be very powerful things in the human mind. The word "end" creates a visual that, for most people, is not very hopeful. How an author finishes a story might create afterthoughts as the reader wonders why something happened or what might have happened next, but you have to remember that there *is* no "end."

That is the beauty of life. Yes, life can seem like a never-ending series of unpleasant or even terrible events. It is also a never-ending series of happy things—the good and the bad, together, are what make up a life. A "life" is an eternal spirit: *There is no end.* That is why you must love and do the right things to bring about "happy endings" for others as well as yourself. That, in my opinion, is what will ultimately make you enjoy your life—or should I say lives?—the most.

Wink! Wink!